HOLLYWOOD DAYS *with* HAYES

HAYES GRIER

HOLLYWOOD DAYS
with HAYES

Feiwel and Friends
New York

A FEIWEL AND FRIENDS BOOK
An imprint of Macmillan Publishing Group, LLC

HOLLYWOOD DAYS WITH HAYES. Copyright © 2016 by Zan Entertainment, Inc.
Photographs on pp. 277–281 courtesy of the author. All rights reserved.
Printed in the United States of America by LSC Communications US, LLC
(Lakeside Classic), Harrisonburg, Virginia. For information, address Feiwel
and Friends, 175 Fifth Avenue, New York, N.Y. 10010.

Our books may be purchased in bulk for promotional, educational, or
business use. Please contact your local bookseller or the Macmillan Corporate
and Premium Sales Department at (800) 221-7945 ext. 5442 or by e-mail at
MacmillanSpecialMarkets@macmillan.com.

Library of Congress Control Number: 2016953279

ISBN 978-1-250-13831-6 (trade paperback) / ISBN 978-1-250-13832-3 (ebook)
10 9 8 7 6 5 4 3 2 1

ISBN 978-1-250-14145-3 (special edition)
10 9 8 7 6 5 4 3 2 1

Book design by Liz Dresner
Feiwel and Friends logo designed by Filomena Tuosto

First Edition—2016

fiercereads.com

HOLLYWOOD DAYS *with* HAYES

PART ONE

Girl Meets Boy

CHAPTER ONE

THE MOVIE SET PULSED WITH ENERGY. Production assistants darted here and there, organizing the soundstage. Crew members set up microphones and rigged lights, figuring out angles and shadows. Props people carted in books, sports posters, and odds and ends for the scene: a typical sixteen-year-old boy's bedroom.

"Hey, dude! Careful with those bowls!" Hayes Grier shouted as someone walked by, balancing a stack of dirty dishes.

The props guy stopped in his tracks. He tensed, looking over at Hayes sitting comfortably off to the side, legs stretched out in front of him, in his director's chair. Then

Hayes grinned, a hey-bro, just-messing-with-you smile. The guy relaxed.

The next second, Hayes jumped up, took some of the bowls, and helped arrange them on the floor next to the rumpled bed. It was only seven a.m., but Hayes had been on set since six, and he was itching to get moving. Besides, he felt bad; he'd probably scared the guy, calling over like he was the director or something.

"Quit fooling around, Hayes." T. J. Meyers, the real director, strode over, checking his watch. "The reporter from *Hollywood This Week* will be here any second."

TJ was only thirty years old, young for a director—especially for a big-budget movie like *The Midnight Hawk*, a film from World Famous Studios, slated to be next summer's blockbuster. At sixteen, Hayes, the movie's star, was even younger. It was a huge responsibility, Hayes knew. A lot was riding on this, for him and for TJ.

Hayes Grier was already famous. He'd been a social media star for years. Vine, YouTube, he felt like he'd put himself out there time and again goofing around with his brother Nash and a big circle of friends . . . competing on *Dancing with the Stars*. But this movie . . . make that, MOVIE! . . . was something else altogether.

How would it change his life? Already it seemed the whole world knew Hayes Grier, and everyone was quick to post a comment.

On his eyes: "Piercing blue." "So deep, you could get lost in them." "He's gotta wear contacts to get them that shade." (Way off-base, Hayes wanted to tell those fans!)

On his straight brown hair: "Love it when it's swept to the side and a little long!"

On his silly antics: "Will he ever win one of those crazy challenges he does with friends? They should try eating crackers and whistling at the same time!"

How would people react to his first movie—and his first starring role? Hayes still couldn't believe it. What could be cooler than this? It didn't even seem real.

"Hayes!" TJ called impatiently, and he was certainly real. *Maybe a little too real*, Hayes thought. The guy was intense!

TJ motioned for Hayes to follow him to the corner, where three chairs had been set up for the interview. Hayes hurried over just as a woman was led over by TJ's assistant, Liza, a cameraman trailing behind.

"Hello." The woman turned to Hayes, smiling. "I'm Alison Portnoy."

She looked familiar, in that "I'm on TV, but you probably can't figure out from where" kind of way. Hayes couldn't guess her age. She could have been anywhere from twenty to fifty, with wavy blond hair, a perky nose, and a nondescript but expensive-looking sleeveless white dress. She waved over her cameraman. "And this is Alex."

"Hi, Alex," Hayes said.

"Alison!" TJ said at the same time, reaching across Hayes to shake the reporter's hand. "Great to see you! Please take a seat."

The three settled into chairs. "If it's all right, I'll talk to the two of you, then take a walk around the set with Alex. I like to have off-the-cuff conversations, nothing rehearsed. So we're ready to go whenever you give the okay."

For Hayes, recording everyday kind of talk was natural, so he nodded. Then he realized Alison wasn't actually asking him; she was asking TJ, who was, of course, the boss.

"It's fine." TJ swept his arm to take in the set. "You realize this is the first day of shooting, though? Things may be a little chaotic."

"Of course." Alison nodded at Alex to begin filming. "I'm just thrilled to be the first to see what's going on here. We'll splice in my introduction later to save time. Alex?"

Alex gave her a thumbs-up, and Alison turned on a smile. "Now I'll start with you, TJ. Just a few questions before I go on to Hayes, so you can leave and take care of business."

"I *am* busy," TJ agreed.

"You've already won an Academy Award for your first film, *A Lighter Shade*. That was a small, independent movie with a shoestring budget. How do you think you'll handle working with almost half a million dollars? And special effects? And a small army of cast and crew members?"

TJ puffed out his chest a bit. "I think I'll handle it just

fine, Alison. *Shade* was my baby from start to finish. This will be, too, but it will actually be easier—I just have to surround myself with intelligent people who get my concepts and ideas and don't need their hands held. Then delegate, delegate, delegate."

"Right," said Alison. She turned to Hayes.

"And of course," TJ went on blithely, "*The Midnight Hawk* will be a huge hit. I personally went over every word in the script, but I can still change anything on the fly, if I feel it's for the good of the movie. And—"

"Speaking of the script," Alison interrupted, "Hayes, why don't you tell us about your character?"

"Sure," said Hayes easily. "I play the title character— Hawk, named after the famous physicist Stephen Hawking, who studies the universe and seems to have so many answers! My movie dad is a scientist, too, and he idolizes him. Hawk doesn't know this yet, but he was really found as a baby under mysterious circumstances—in the middle of a large empty field within a perfect circle of scorched grass."

"Hmmm," Alison put in. "Interesting. A hawk is a beautiful, graceful creature. You fit the description perfectly."

"Um." Hayes blushed. He wanted to talk about the role, not his looks.

"Yes, that was a nice bit of casting," TJ added before Hayes could say a word. "I put a lot of thought into finding the right actor. I was looking for a fresh face. Someone without a lot of acting experience; someone I could mold into my own vision. Hayes didn't mention that Hawk turns out to be an alien, left behind when his spacecraft left the field, hence the scorched ground and ashes. That was actually my little addition, the character's name and movie title."

"Right." Alison nodded, a little curtly. "How do you feel about carrying a movie?" she asked Hayes. "It is your very first movie role, after all."

"He's excited to be working with me," TJ answered quickly.

"Hayes?" Alison shifted in her seat to face him directly.

"Well, I am excited to work with TJ, of course. I'm excited to have this opportunity. My fans have been so supportive. I want to show them another side of me, outside social media. A serious side, taking on a role that requires real talent. I don't want to let them down."

He paused. "And the people here have been amazing, too. I mean, it's all been incredible . . . the crew, the sets, the script . . . I still can't believe I'm part of this."

Alison nodded encouragingly. "You seem almost humbled by this experience, Hayes."

"That's it!" Hayes sat up straight. "I—"

"We," TJ corrected. "We all feel humbled to work on this project. It's an opportunity for all of us. This movie will be a box office smash. And when I'm done, I can—I mean we can—go on to any project we choose. You do know I'm getting a producer credit as well? It's a tall order, being behind the camera, but also being in charge of every aspect of a major production . . ."

TJ kept talking and Hayes nodded along, smiling. Doing press was part of the deal, he understood, and he'd do everything he could to be professional about the whole thing, even if TJ was running off at the mouth. Besides, he loved *A Lighter Shade*. Clearly, TJ knew what he was doing. He glanced at the bedroom set, finished and ready for filming, the bowls right where he'd left them. He was ready, too.

Fifteen miles from World Famous Studios, in Venice, California, a bedroom door opened slowly. Violet Reeves burrowed deeper under the soft fluffy blanket. "Five more minutes, Mom," she pleaded sleepily. "Just five more minutes, then I'll get up for school."

Violet tensed, ready for her mom to pull off the blanket, like she did most mornings. Instead, there was silence. *Hmmm*, she thought, drifting off again. *Maybe I dreamed that someone opened the door.* She sniffed the air. *Like I'm dreaming this funny smell.*

Bit by bit, the smell grew stronger. It reminded Violet of

burning leaves. She snuggled into the pillow, remembering fall days when she was little and her dad would rake leaves into a pile, then light a match and . . . Burning leaves? She sat bolt upright. This was no dream. Was there a fire?

"Relax, honey."

"Uncle Forrest? What's going on?" Violet rubbed her eyes, trying to get herself together. She wasn't home with her parents in upstate New York. She was in California, spending the summer with her uncle and cousin, Mia.

"It's the first day of the month, my ritual Smudge Day," Uncle Forrest explained.

"Smudge," Violet repeated, falling back on the pillow.

"I'm cleansing the house of all negativity using this smudge wand, and your room is first on my list."

Her uncle held up some sort of stick, and Violet peered closer. The stick was really a bunch of white leaves twisted together, held in place by a bright red string. Smoke billowed from one end, filling the air with a not-unpleasant scent.

"White sage." Uncle Forrest steadied a large seashell under the wand to catch falling ashes. He stepped closer to show Violet. "Uh-oh," he said as the smoke swelled. "The thicker the smoke, the greater the negativity."

He waved the wand back and forth over Violet's bed. She watched him warily, hoping he wouldn't set the blanket on fire.

"This will restore balance and freshness. Begone, bad vibes," he cried. "Begone!"

Violet was used to her uncle's New Age philosophies and his spiritual take on the world, not to mention the way he dressed. Right now he was wearing a tie-dyed shirt and overalls, his graying hair tied back in a ponytail.

He and her mom had grown up in Chicago, but they'd moved in opposite directions—Uncle Forrest to the West Coast, her mom to the East and a law career in a small town. Still, they had their similarities: Violet's mom leaned toward granola and locally sourced food, with an almost superstitious view of life. She chose Violet's name to make sure her eyes stayed the same violet shade she was born with, and they did. So Violet figured maybe there was something to this mystical take on things.

Thinking of her mom, Violet smiled and stretched happily, luxuriating in the knowledge there'd be no school, and no rude blanket-pulling.

It still seemed unbelievable to her. But here she was, living in this amazing place, just steps away from Venice Beach and the Pacific Ocean. She'd visited before, of course. She loved Venice—the walk streets, pedestrian-only walkways tucked behind homes and businesses; the famed boardwalk with its colorful murals, street performers, and vendors. Even better, her cousin, Mia, the same age as Violet—sixteen—was really and truly her BFF. All year long they texted, Snapchatted, and talked, and now they'd be living together for weeks and weeks. How lucky could one person be?

Yes, she was lucky, but Violet had worked hard to get here, too. For as long as she could remember, Violet loved movies. She loved everything about them, from opening credits to closing credits. She loved them all—from thrillers to musicals. From dramas to boy-meets-girl movies, where the story always followed the same formula: Boy meets girl. Boy almost gets girl but something happens, driving them apart. Then, finally, boy gets girl and a happy ending.

Like that would ever happen in real life, Violet told herself.

But out of all the genres, Violet had a special weakness for movies about making movies, because that's what she wanted to do: make movies, or more specifically, write them. She wanted to create characters that would come alive on-screen, and see her story ideas play out like real life.

That spring, she'd entered a writing competition. It wasn't her first, not by a long shot. This time, though, she'd spent weeks on the idea, then weeks on the first draft, and weeks on the second, polishing dialogue, tinkering with stage directions. And she'd won! The prize: an internship on a Hollywood movie set. Unbelievable!

"And now for the daily Earth Blessing." Uncle Forrest interrupted her thoughts. Unlike the smudging, this was totally expected. Almost every morning, Uncle Forrest had

Violet repeat his own, personally created blessing: a phrase he came up with, designed to bring guidance and happiness. And Violet was totally up for a little guidance and happiness.

"Today," he intoned.

"Today," Violet repeated.

"I express my gratitude to the planet."

"I express my gratitude to the planet."

"I breathe in all of nature and breathe out my thanks."

"Same."

"Violet," Uncle Forrest said sternly.

"Okay, okay." So much for moving things along. "I breathe in all of nature and breathe out my thanks."

Violet took a moment to feel at peace, then asked, "What time is it, Uncle Forrest?"

"Time?" He looked at her quizzically. "You know I don't keep track of that. Time is an artificial constraint of the mind."

As he lectured, Violet reached for her phone on the nightstand. "Eight o'clock!" she screeched.

"Eight o'clock, three o'clock, or midnight. It's all meaningless. Time does not really exist," Uncle Forrest went on in soothing tones.

"I bet it exists to T. J. Meyers!" Violet exclaimed. TJ was her new boss. She didn't know him very well, but she guessed he would not be happy if she was late on her very first day of work.

Hurriedly, Violet grabbed some clothes, dressed in the bathroom, and then bounded downstairs, almost tripping down the floating staircase, its glass steps seemingly suspended in midair. At the bottom, she paused only long enough to pull her long reddish-brown curls into a ponytail.

In the kitchen, Violet saw Mia sitting at the table. As usual, Mia's head was bent over a sketchbook, her short blond hair falling into her eyes.

Mia still wore her robe, a Japanese kimono with long billowing sleeves that swept the page when she moved the pencil. She wasn't quite like her dad. But she was definitely a free spirit, dressing in an offbeat but somehow chic way that Violet couldn't imagine pulling off.

Violet glanced down at her own slim dark jeans and formfitting white button-down blouse. Not exactly cutting-edge, she knew. But she was going to her first real job and didn't want to go overboard either way; too out there, or too casual.

Violet was really late now, but she couldn't resist peeking over Mia's shoulder.

On the page, Mia was drawing a loose-fitting minidress, with a deep V-neck and a flared bottom.

"Violet!" Mia exclaimed. "You're still here? I thought you would have left before I woke up."

"I know, I know!" Violet grabbed a glass. "I'm always so punctual. If I'm on time, I think I'm late! But I overslept."

"Dad's nightly drum circle must have kept you up last night." Mia pushed the orange juice container closer to Violet. Violet poured quickly, her hand trembling with nerves and excitement. The juice splashed the table, narrowly missing her white shirt.

"Oh God," she said, wiping up the mess. "That's right! I was up half the night with that banging and chanting. What were they chanting for? It sounded like they were saying, 'Pest control! Pest control!'"

Mia laughed. "It was 'rent control.' They want to heal themselves—and the community—with affordable housing. It's actually a good idea. It's hard to live around here if you're not a millionaire." She eyed Violet sympathetically as she banged around the kitchen, opening and closing cabinets, trying to find something to eat.

"Maybe Uncle Forrest should have chanted for some cereal," Violet mumbled. "Oh, you know I don't mean that!" She swirled around to face Mia. "You guys have been nothing but nice to me!"

"It's okay, Violet. You're so frazzled right now, you probably don't even know what you're saying. Listen, I'll drive you to work. In fact," Mia said, standing up and closing her sketchbook, "I'll start the car while you grab something to eat for the ride."

She took a few steps, came back for her sketchbook, then hurried outside, the car keys swinging in her hand.

"Aha!" Violet said, opening the small cabinet above the refrigerator. "A muffin!" She read the label. *Gluten free matcha muffin.* Wasn't that made from green tea?

She had no idea how it would taste. But it would have to do.

CHAPTER TWO

main character

"HURRY, HURRY!" VIOLET TOLD HERSELF, practically running to the driveway. "I can't be late on my very first day!" The car, a sporty-looking two-door about a decade old, was already turned on, and Mia was waving out the window.

"Coming!" Violet shouted, not paying attention to anything but the car and Mia.

"Good morning!" called someone from next door.

Violet twisted her head toward the voice and crashed into some drums Uncle Forrest had left outside.

"Whoa!" Violet held out her hands to stop her fall and landed on her side with a thud. For a moment, she didn't move.

"That's right! Stay right there! Don't move until you're sure you're okay." A boy who looked about her age, maybe a little older, rushed over. He bent over her anxiously. "That was totally my fault! I shouldn't have called out to you when you were running! Can you stand up?" He held out his hand.

Violet gazed up at him. He was definitely cute, with curly blondish hair and a sweet, concerned expression. But why was she even noticing? She was late!

Violet jumped to her feet, not bothering to answer. "Oh no! Is my shirt okay?" she called out to Mia. "Are there any stains?" She twisted around, trying to see her sides and back. She probably sounded like an idiot, but she didn't care. "Where's my backpack? Did I drop it? Oh no! I didn't even bring it!"

She raced inside and when she got back out, the boy was still there. "I'm Jay," he offered. He was holding Violet's muffin, miraculously still intact. "Don't forget this. Lucky for you, it landed right-side up! And you must be Violet. Mia told me you were coming." He grinned lazily at her. "Do you always go one-hundred miles per hour?"

Violet stopped short, taking the muffin. Was this boy flirting with her? When clearly she had places she had to be and was in no mood for small talk?

"You should slow down and smell the roses." The boy

took a few steps, then plucked a rose from his yard and held it out to her. "Life is short."

"What?" Violet almost screeched, ignoring the flower. Everyone knew the worst thing to tell a panicked person was to slow down or stay calm. "I don't have time to smell anything! I'm late!" And she jumped into the car, slamming the door behind her.

Mia waved, then backed out of the driveway. They drove in silence for a few minutes, Violet munching on the muffin. *Not bad*, she thought. *And healthy, too.* She began to feel calmer.

She looked at the car clock. 8:27. She still had to pick up coffee for TJ—her very first task—and be at the lot at 9. It was really cutting it close.

"So you met Jay," Mia said, breaking into her thoughts.

"What? Who?"

"Jay. Our neighbor. He's seventeen."

"Oh yeah. Jay."

Mia glanced over at Violet. "You must be nervous. Jay is really cute, and you didn't notice?"

"I did notice," Violet admitted. "But this summer is definitely not for romance. I have to concentrate on my job."

The job, Violet thought, that would bring her in close proximity to one Hayes Grier, her number one celebrity crush. She'd been trying to block it out, to focus on writing and interning for TJ. But somehow, that fact kept creeping in.

What were the chances she'd even see Hayes? There were thousands of people working on the movie, dozens of locations, and different sets. Surely, she'd be on the nonglamorous end of things, doing grunt work, probably for the writers or TJ. If she was lucky, she'd spy Hayes from a distance. And really, that was just as well. How could she concentrate if he was close by?

"It *is* a big job," Mia agreed.

"I haven't even told you the best part," Violet said, wiping her mouth with a tissue she found in the glove compartment. "I only had to submit one scene for this writing contest. But I spent all last year writing an entire script. When I FaceTimed with TJ for my interview, he said he'd read the whole thing and give me feedback."

Mia merged onto the Santa Monica Freeway, then patted Violet's knee. "And?"

"Well, I'm meeting with him first thing. And if he liked my script? He'll write me a college recommendation letter to get into the Hollywood Screenwriting Academy!"

"The Academy?" Mia whistled. "That's the most selective school in California! I've heard it's even harder to get into than Harvard!"

Violet groaned. "I know. And I have to apply in the fall!

If he doesn't write that rec for me, it doesn't leave much time to get another one."

"I'm sure he loved it," Mia said loyally.

"Well, it could be the best screenplay since *Gone with the Wind*. But if I'm late for work, that wouldn't make the slightest bit of difference. TJ would still toss it and refuse to write the letter. I don't think TJ's the easiest guy to work for. His assistant told me *he* can be late, but he hates if anyone else is. Even one minute late drives him crazy. And I can't forget to pick up a coffee for him on the way in."

Violet tapped her phone to look at her notes. "A coconut-almond iced cappuccino with a scoop of condensed milk spiced with juniper and basil. Who knows how long that even takes to make!"

They pulled up to World Famous Studios, choosing the first gate they came to. Mia gave Violet's name, and the guard waved them through. But inside, Mia braked uncertainly. The studio looked like a busy city, with streets branching off in different directions, and golf carts zipping around them.

"Oh God. It's 8:54," Violet moaned. "We'll never find the right soundstage."

"Have a little faith!" Mia said cheerfully. She rolled down her window and asked the first person who walked past, a man herding a crowd of people dressed like cavemen and cavewomen. "Excuse me, but do you know where they're filming *The Midnight Hawk*?"

The man nodded. "Take a left up ahead, then two quick rights."

"Thanks!" Mia said, already pulling away. One minute later, she stopped again, outside a large building where a stream of people hurried in and out. "This must be it. And look!" She pointed across the street to a coffee cart parked at the corner.

"That's a sign things will work out!" Mia cried as Violet flung open the door. "It's 8:55. You have plenty of time."

Hayes had been on set for three hours. First he'd been rushed through hair and wardrobe like it was some kind of cosmetic emergency. And at the end? He thought he wound up looking very close to his normal self. Then an assistant director had hurried him to set for the *Hollywood This Week* interview, where he'd sat around waiting for so long, his makeup had to be retouched.

It was a lot of action, with very little to show for it.

Now, for the past hour or so, he'd done nothing but hang around while an assistant director walked through shots with his stand-in, making sure to get the right camera angles.

With nothing else going on, Hayes lounged in the director's chair and went over the interview in his head. He sighed. It hadn't gone very well, he thought, at least on his end. With TJ going on and on about his work, his ideas, his movie, Hayes barely got to say a word. Maybe the reporter would forget Hayes was even the star and cut him from the clip.

Hayes knew he was being silly. Publicity should be the least of his concerns. He was here for the work. He should forget about being a celebrity, about being famous. He needed to concentrate on being the best actor possible. That was the important thing: the work.

He was just getting antsy, that's all. Hopefully, they'd film this scene before he was old enough to vote, and once they started, he'd feel better.

The scene they were shooting came pretty early in the movie. But it was far from the first one. It seemed shooting was always out of order. TJ wanted to film scenes in a group, set by set. First they'd shoot his bedroom scenes, then the school cafeteria ones, and so on. But it was all a little confusing, so Hayes ran through the early scenes in his head, keeping everything in order.

The beginning scenes took place in school, with "Hawk" getting the courage to ask out "Devon," who would become his girlfriend. Then came a few shots at a pizza place and movie theater.

The scene in his bedroom came after: Hawk is lying in bed, goofing around on his phone when his mom comes in. She's clearly upset, torn about whether to tell him something. Finally, she brings out an old photo album and shows him baby pictures, then shots of finding him in that scorched field.

Hawk is shocked beyond belief. He's adopted, just picked up in some strange field! He'd had no idea. Then he learns something more: He's not even a human child! He's an alien.

Hawk doesn't think it can get any worse, but it does. His mom shows him his father's journal. His dad is a scientist, and he's been trying to find out what makes Hawk different from humans. There are notations on his growth, his speech patterns, and his intelligence, starting at three months and ending last week.

The last entry stated observation was not enough. Previous findings had proven inconclusive. Hawk would be taken to a laboratory, held under lock and key, while his dad ran test after test. He'd be a prisoner. Everyone would be told he'd been killed in a motorcycle crash.

"Run," his movie mom tells him. "Run."

"Run," Hayes repeated to himself. "I should run through these lines again."

He looked around the set. Everyone was busy doing something . . . something important, he guessed. He couldn't just pull somebody over and demand they help with his lines. Normally, his assistant—and buddy—Jackson would be right there with him, happy to help. But Jackson had just switched to a new job yesterday, running Hayes's online merchandise store, and he couldn't do both. It was a big job, handling the website, keeping track of T-shirts and hoodies, coming up with new ideas for merch.

Hayes liked the idea of a bobblehead, but that would have to be looked into.

Hayes stood up. He definitely needed a new assistant, and not just for lines. He needed all the help he could get.

Scoping out TJ, he waited for the director to be alone. Then he quickly walked over. "Hey, TJ, got a minute?"

"Not really," TJ muttered. Then he looked at his watch. "Well, I have to take a break in a bit anyway, to meet with an intern, so why don't we take our usual seats?" He waved to the set of interview chairs, and Hayes sat back down.

While Hayes told TJ about Jackson and his need for a new assistant, TJ scrolled through his phone, shouted at people passing by, and drank his coffee. He tossed the cup into a wastebasket and sighed, looking around as if another would magically appear.

"Have you even been listening?" Hayes asked in exasperation.

"Sure," TJ said, his eyes finally meeting Hayes's. "You need a new assistant. Don't worry. I'll find you one."

"Great!" Hayes grinned. "That's really great."

"In the meantime," TJ went on, "I have some news for you."

Now that he had TJ's full attention, Hayes almost took out his own phone, to show him what it felt like to have someone half-listen. But he didn't. Getting back at the director wasn't quite the professional thing to do. "What's up?"

"There's been a change in the script."

"Is it major?"

"Kind of," TJ answered. "There's a new ending."

Hayes's heart sank. He'd been hoping *The Midnight Hawk* would turn out to be the first in a series. "Tell me you don't kill off Hawk."

"Nope," TJ said cheerfully. "You get to live. And you still get to beat the bad guys."

"So what changes? Is the big motorcycle stunt still in? Or did you cut it?"

Getting rid of that scene and Hawk's supercharged ride would be almost as bad as dying.

TJ shook his head. "That's in, too. But we changed the last scene. You break up with Devon at the very end. You love her. But you want to protect her. If she stays with you, she's in danger from your enemies."

TJ thrust new script pages at Hayes. Hayes quickly scanned them: Devon is tearful. She tells him she knew all along he didn't really love her—at least not enough to stand by her. The last shot is Hawk standing alone on a hill, overlooking the city. A single tear rolls down his cheek. Then he squares his shoulders and turns, ready to take on the world.

"It's pretty emotional," TJ was saying. "Do you think you can handle it?"

Hayes looked up and met his eyes. "Of course," he said easily. "It sounds like a great scene. Not a problem, TJ."

"Good." TJ checked his phone. "Why don't you go back to your trailer and relax? It turns out we won't need you until this afternoon."

Hayes nodded. He'd have to go through hair and makeup again. That was annoying. But maybe it was a good thing. He needed time to digest this news. Crying on camera? Showing a vulnerable side on-screen? He'd sounded confident to TJ.

But that's not how he felt at all.

Violet glanced at her phone as she rushed onto set. 9:01. One minute late. But she had the coffee, and she'd even picked up fruit-salad-in-a-cup to go with the drink. Who doesn't like fruit? Sure, it was a brownnose move to appease TJ. But maybe it would help.

Suddenly, Violet stopped, not sure where to find TJ. People rushed past her. Everyone wore an intense expression, and she didn't want to bother anyone with a silly question. Then she spied the bedroom, with cameras surrounding the scene. Maybe TJ would be around there.

Violet edged her way over, losing even more precious seconds. It was 9:02 now. Where was he?

"There you are!" came a loud voice behind her. Violet spun around, the coffee sloshing over the cup lid and dripping down her arm. She ignored it.

"TJ!" she exclaimed. "Here's the coffee! And I brought you some fruit, too."

The director ran a hand through his short spiky hair and frowned, but took the offerings. "You're three minutes late."

Violet held back from correcting him. It was still only two.

"I'm so sorry. There was a line for the—"

"I'm not interested in excuses," he cut in. "Part of your job is to be punctual. Time is money while we film. We have everything planned to the second."

"Excuse me, TJ?" a nervous production assistant interrupted. "But we have to push back the bedroom scene until at least one o'clock. The crew finished filming those rain forest location shots, but they're stuck in Seattle."

"Guess you can't plan everything!" Violet said without thinking. She flushed, realizing she should have kept quiet.

TJ nodded brusquely and steered Violet to the director's chairs. There were three. Violet stood there awkwardly, unwilling to sit in the ones marked HAYES or TJ, and she couldn't see the name on the third. What if it was for the actor who played the bad guy? He was big and scary, and he had a really big name, too.

"Here!" TJ pushed the chair in front of her. The back was

blank. Gratefully, she sank down. Then she remembered she was on the job. She edged forward and sat up straight, hoping she looked capable.

"I'll be up front with you, Victoria."

"Violet."

"What? Oh yeah, Violet. I read your script, and I didn't like it."

Violet deflated, her hopes dashed. Would that be it? Would she spend the summer getting coffee and fruit cups, then be on her merry way without a letter of recommendation? And no chance of getting into the Academy?

TJ didn't seem to notice her change in posture. "Your writing voice is weak; it's barely there. You need to have a stronger, more singular style. You need a better POV."

"POV?" Violet repeated weakly.

"Point of view," TJ went on briskly. "There's no heart in your script. And that's what's most important." He tapped his chest. "Heart."

He sounded so cold and unfeeling. *He* could use some heart. But she nodded. She stood up, convinced the meeting was over.

"Now hold on a second." TJ waved her back down. "Your writing has problems. Big ones, too. I can't write that rec."

Okay, Violet got all that. Why was he still talking?

"But," he continued, "I do see potential."

Violet sucked in her breath and waited to hear more.

"I'm willing to read another script."

"B-b-but," Violet stammered, "I don't have another script."

"You will," TJ said. "At the end of the summer, by the time *The Midnight Hawk* has its premiere."

The end of the summer? It had taken Violet months to write the first one, the one without heart or point of view. How could she possibly write a whole other—better—one so fast?

Still, it was a chance. She had more direction now. Plus, shadowing TJ around set, learning the ins and outs of dialogue would certainly help!

"Thank you so much!" Violet gushed.

"You are welcome. As I said, I'm willing to read the script . . . under certain conditions."

There were more conditions, besides that ridiculous deadline?

"I'm changing your job, as of right now. You are no longer my intern. You are Hayes Grier's assistant."

"I am?" Violet felt her pulse quicken. This couldn't really be happening. She wouldn't be shadowing TJ after all. She'd be working for Hayes Grier!

"Yes. But I warn you, it won't be easy. You'll have to get every little thing right. You'll need to make sure Hayes is always on time. That he knows his lines and doesn't do anything stupid. The boy needs to buckle down and stay safe. If he does any crazy tricks on that scooter or does anything that could put him in harm's way, not only will he be hurt, but the movie will be hurt, too. Your job is to make sure that doesn't happen. So if you do all that? Then, and only then, will I read your new script."

He paused. "Do we have a deal?"

Violet's head was spinning. It was almost too much to wrap her mind around—she had another chance for a recommendation . . . she had to write a new script . . . she would be Hayes Grier's new assistant . . . and no matter how starstruck she felt, she had to do everything right.

"I repeat, do we have a deal?"

Violet took a deep breath. "Yes!"

CHAPTER THREE

VIOLET STOOD OUTSIDE HAYES'S TRAILER. One thin wall separated her from her celebrity crush.

So, you have a crush on Hayes, she told herself, trying to be reasonable. *What girl doesn't?*

Every girl wanted to date Hayes Grier. And every guy wanted to be part of his bro squad. Voices filtered through the trailer door—the squad in the flesh.

One part of Violet wanted to rush inside and meet everyone. The other part wanted to run away and hide.

Slowly Violet raised her hand. She forced herself to knock. No one answered. The voices had grown louder, and no one had heard. She knocked again harder. Still no answer. Finally, she swung open the door.

Violet stood on the step, frozen in place, staring inside. There he was—the one and only Hayes Grier—sitting on a couch, directly facing her, a surprised look in his eyes.

The room fell silent. Four guys and one dog gawked at her, waiting for her to speak.

"Hi!" she squeaked.

"Hello," Hayes said, making it sound like a question.

"I'm Violet, your new assistant."

"Oh, hi, Violet!" Hayes stood up. "I'm Hayes."

Like she didn't know!

"And this is Tez." Violet knew who Tez was, too, from the YouTube videos: Hayes's best friend. He introduced the others, Jake and Duncan.

Violet, still standing at the door like an idiot, nodded at them all. But thankfully, Hayes led her over to Zan, his dog. "And I'd like you to meet my best bud, Zan."

Violet crouched to scratch the adorable black Lab behind the ears. "Oh, he's so cute."

"So you like dogs?" Hayes asked.

"Yes, I love you," Violet said. She clapped a hand over her mouth. Did she just say she loved Hayes Grier? "I mean I love dogs! Dogs! I love dogs!" She felt her cheeks grow warm. She must be bright red. This had to be the most embarrassing thing ever.

"*Oooooh!*" said Tez. "Seems like somebody in this room is in love!"

"Yeah," said Jake, making smooching noises. "Violet is in *luuuuv* with Hayes."

"Hayes and Violet sitting in a tree," Duncan sang out. "K-i-s-s-i-n-g!"

How old were these boys? Eight or nine? Violet should just ignore them, continue talking with Hayes, and nail down her duties. But it was hard. They were so loud—and annoying!

"Let's exchange cell phone numbers," she told Hayes, trying to block out the oohs and aahs and comments about flirting by text. She raised her still-shaky voice. "So you can let me know if you need anything."

"Sure," said Hayes. "I actually could use some help with a few errands. I already have a list." He sounded almost apologetic as he handed her a scribbled-on piece of paper.

This was good. Now, thank goodness, she could leave. "Thanks so much," she said, realizing a beat too late it was a stupid thing to say. Who thanks someone for giving them chores?

Hurriedly, she turned to go, eager to get outside and calm down and—*smack*! She walked right into a wall.

All the guys broke up, laughing.

"Hey, who put a wall in this trailer?" she tried to joke, then slipped out as quickly as she could. Outside, she raced down the street, then slumped by a fence. What a way to start her new job! Embarrassment aside, she'd come across as totally incompetent. What if she was like this—starstruck and silly—for the rest of the shoot? She'd be a terrible assistant. TJ would never read her script!

That afternoon, Violet once again stood outside Hayes's trailer. She'd just gotten back from craft services with Hayes's lunch—turkey on rye with Swiss, mayo, coleslaw, and arugula salad—along with lots of chips, pretzels, and cookies. She crossed *food* off Hayes's list. Then she went through the other items, making sure she'd taken care of every request.

Pick up tomorrow's outfit from wardrobe.

Check.

She'd already put the clothes in Hayes's closet.

Send pictures of the trailer and cute shots of Zan to friends and family.

Check.

She'd used her own phone for that request, along with Hayes's contact list.

Organize fan mail.

Check.

She'd pushed a cart full of mail to a table off to the side. Then she'd placed the letters into piles: Sweet ones. Crazy ones. Long ones. Short ones.

No one had told her how to do it. She'd pretty much made up her own categories. She hoped she'd made the right decisions.

Violet sighed. It was hard enough finding her way around the lot, never mind figuring out how to actually do the errands. And everything had to be done absolutely perfectly. Her recommendation letter was on the line.

Of course, she'd already messed up, embarrassing herself in front of Hayes. If that happened again—in any way, shape, or form—she would just die.

This time, their meeting had to go better!

Still feeling hesitant, Violet raised her hand, ready to rap on the trailer door. When she heard Hayes's voice, she stopped in midair. Oh no! She couldn't go in while his friends were there. She really, really didn't want to see them. On the other hand, she couldn't be late with the sandwich and snacks. It was such a small thing, and seemed so silly, but she didn't know what to do.

Finally, she made a decision: She'd just wait a bit and hope the friends would leave. She turned away, looking for a spot to hide, when she realized only Hayes was talking. No one was answering.

She leaned closer to the door, trying to hear his words.

"You are such a good puppy," Hayes was saying. "Aren't you, boy? My best buddy, my best friend in the world. I wouldn't trade you for a million dollars. For a jet plane. For a starring role in the biggest blockbuster of all time! You know that, don't you, Zan?"

Hayes was talking to his dog! And he was being so sweet, so playful. Violet's heart melted. She smiled. Really, she couldn't be nervous with a guy who talked to his dog— even if it was world-famous Hayes Grier. She felt herself relax.

Violet knocked twice. This time she waited for Hayes's "Come in!" Then she walked inside.

"Violet!" Hayes was parked in front of the wide-screen TV, watching last night's Lakers game. Zan was stretched out next to him, his chin on Hayes's knee.

The first time she'd been in the trailer, Violet had been too nervous to look around. Since then, she'd been back on her own, and she'd already noted the TV, the full kitchen and living room, and the good-sized bedroom off to the side. It seemed like a classy apartment, and once again she marveled that it was really just a trailer.

"I'm taking a break," Hayes told her, "watching yesterday's game. Don't tell me who wins! I want to watch the whole thing like it's live. Man, I can't stand those Celtics."

Violet had no idea who won, or even that there'd been a game. "Okay," she agreed. "I won't."

Suddenly, Hayes clicked off the TV. "Ah, it doesn't matter anyway. It's nearly over. And I want to talk to you." He patted the couch.

Violet slid next to him, leaving plenty of space between them, and perched on the edge of the cushion. "Should I take notes?" she asked.

"No, it's nothing like that." Hayes took a deep breath. "I want to say I'm sorry. My buddies were acting like jerks before. Really, they're nicer than they seem. But there's no excuse. They were way out of line, and I didn't do anything to stop them. I feel terrible."

Violet started to say something, but Hayes held up his hand.

"I thought if I spoke up, it would turn into a bigger deal—you know, they'd be all like '*Ooh*, Hayes is standing up for his girlfriend. *Oooooh!*' And I'd have made the whole thing worse, embarrassing you even more. But I don't think they were funny or anything. And I do feel really bad."

Violet's face turned red just thinking about the earlier meeting. But she didn't blame Hayes. Not at all.

"It's okay. And you're right. If you'd said anything, it would have made them go on and on even more, and really, all I wanted to do was get out of this trailer."

"Whew!" Hayes grinned. "That's a relief. I was worried you thought I was a jerk, too."

Hayes was worried about how *she* felt? He was just as nice in real life as he was in all of his videos. It wasn't an act.

"I didn't think that at all," she assured him. "But are those guys coming back?" She glanced at the door just as it swung open hard, banging against the wall.

"Hayes, my handsome young star!" A woman dressed all in black, with the highest heels Violet had ever seen, strode into the trailer. She flashed a smile at Hayes, ignored Violet, and headed right for the snacks Violet had placed on the table. She dipped a chip in guacamole, popped it in her mouth, and then planted herself inches in front of Hayes.

"Have you met my new assistant, Violet?" Hayes asked.

"Hello, dear," the woman said, not turning her head. "Now, Hayes, how did the first day of shooting go?"

Hayes jumped to his feet, excited to talk about it. "Everyone crushed it! The entire cast and crew! I mean, we had to wait a long time to get going. And we did about a hundred takes of that scene between my mom and me. But I think we got some really good stuff."

He waved his arm to include Violet in the conversation. "This is Selena Young, the movie's publicist."

"Nice to meet—"

"Now, Hayes," Selena went on as if Violet hadn't spoken at all. "I have a new call sheet for you. We've reordered tomorrow's schedule to accommodate your trip."

Violet knew publicists arrange celebrity appearances. Their job was to get good press for their clients. Just being in on a conversation like this was amazing!

"The Children's Hospital is expecting you first thing in the morning," Selena finished.

"Oh, that's great. Thanks, Selena. I've already been in touch with these kids, and I can't wait to meet them. Some of them have been in the hospital for weeks. I'm wondering if I should bring them anything. You know, books or movies or—"

"Hmmm," Selena said, going through her phone. "It seems Harris Gold from *YMT* will get to the hospital a little late."

YMT was short for *Your Movie Ticket*, a major film magazine. Violet read it religiously.

"No matter," Selena continued. "There will be plenty of other reporters to cover your visit."

"Cover my visit?" Hayes repeated. "What do you mean?"

"Why, Hayes, sweetie, I thought you realized. I've invited tons of reporters to be there. It's an event! Just think! 'Hayes Grier Brings His Own Special Medicine to Sick Children,' or some sort of fluff like that. Readers will eat it up. You'll have to bring posters of *The Midnight Hawk* to autograph. That would really get the word out.

"Now let's figure out what you should wear—something casual or a little more dressy? Or maybe you should go in character. That would promote the movie big time."

Selena reached for another chip, but Hayes closed the bag. "Selena! You invited reporters? I thought you were just helping me out, to make the filming schedule go smoother for everyone. I didn't know you were turning this into a huge promotion!"

Selena moved breezily on to the pretzels. "Well, that's just how things work, Hayes."

"Not for me," Hayes said firmly. "I've never had reporters trailing me when I'm trying to help people. And I don't want to start now. I just want to meet these kids. They follow me on Twitter and Instagram and feel like they know me. I don't want a bunch of reporters getting in the way."

"But think of the positive press!" Selena persisted. "The photo ops! How about I just tip off one of the paparazzi—maybe Greta Gleason. She's only five feet tall. No one will even notice her! And if they do, she can say she's visiting a patient. Nobody will know we invited her. It's perfect!" She tapped her phone, making some notes.

Hayes closed the pretzel bag. Violet jumped up and put all the snacks in the kitchen cabinets. Hayes shot her a grateful look.

"I said no, Selena," Hayes said, sounding annoyed. "And I meant it. I don't feel comfortable with an 'entourage'"— he put the word in air quotes—"especially when I'm trying to make a difference. Real charity is what happens when no one is watching. This is not a photo op, a media story, or anything image-related. It's me and some fans. And if there's just one picture or story—even a single line—in a paper, magazine, or online, I'm done. I mean it, Selena. I'll walk away from this movie."

He paused, catching his breath.

"It may not always seem that way, but I like my privacy. Parts of my life need to stay private."

Violet, still in the kitchen, tried to make herself as small as possible. She didn't want to get in the way. What if Selena didn't back down and Hayes really quit? She never thought a celebrity would be so casual with fame and starring roles. But apparently, Hayes was.

He stood up for what he believed was right.

Violet snuck an admiring glance at him. He wasn't only funny and personable and adorable. Far from it. He was strong and honorable. A good person.

Hayes walked over to the door and held it open for Selena. "So what do you say?" he asked.

"I say you win, Hayes darling," Selena said as she swept out. "No press at the Children's Hospital. But just think about taking those movie posters with you!"

Hayes closed the door, then smiled at Violet. "And what do you say, Violet *dahling*?" He stretched out the word like a phony-sounding celebrity. Then he switched to his normal voice. "Want to bring out those snacks again and watch the rest of the game with me?"

CHAPTER FOUR

LATE THAT AFTERNOON, Hayes insisted Violet take a cab back to Venice, on him. When she walked up the steps to the house, Mia flung open the door. "I've been waiting for you!" she cried, pulling Violet inside. "You didn't answer any of my texts. How was it? What did the director say? Did you get a glimpse of Hayes Grier?"

"Slow down!" Violet plopped onto the living room couch. She kicked off her shoes. "I'll tell you everything. Just give me a minute."

"No! Now!" Mia demanded. "You know it's only because I love you! I care about you!"

"Okay, okay. It's all about me. You don't care about Hayes Grier at all." Violet laughed, then quickly filled Mia in on the day: the bad news about TJ and her script. The good news about the second chance he'd give if she could write another, better one. Then the deal: take on the job of Hayes's assistant, keeping him in line, on time, and safe and sound.

For a moment, Mia was shocked into silence. Her mouth actually hung open, like someone who'd just walked in to a surprise party.

"You're acting so weird," Violet said to her. "Like you're freaked out about Hayes. I thought you didn't care about celebrity stuff."

Mia was Venice Beach–cool, into art and design, not gossip or blockbuster movies with billion-dollar budgets and the newest "it" stars. She went to small, intimate films shown in out-of-the-way theaters. Violet had seen her walk past teen idols without giving them a second look.

"For your information, I'm acting perfectly normal," Mia told her haughtily. "I just want to ask a few questions, if you don't mind. What was he wearing? What were his first words to you? Did he seem like the same person from the videos? Did he say anything about *Dancing with the Stars*?"

An hour later, Violet had answered all of Mia's questions and filled her in on the Hayes and Selena standoff. Now she was truly exhausted. And hungry, too, she realized. Those chips and pretzels could only keep a person going for so long.

"Any plan for dinner?" she asked Mia.

"Well, there is a little something planned," Mia said with a grin. "How would you like to have a picnic on the beach with Jay and some of his friends?"

Jay? It took a few seconds for Violet to put it together. The guy from this morning, the neighbor who'd helped her up when she'd tripped. It seemed like it happened a lifetime ago.

Violet stretched. She felt like she'd run a marathon. How many times had she raced from one end of the lot to the other today? Maybe she *had* run a marathon!

"I don't know," she told Mia. "It's been a long day, and I still have plenty to do."

"Come on, it will be fun. Dad is out, and this way you won't have to think about dinner."

"Let me see what's in the fridge." Violet walked into the kitchen. She opened the refrigerator door and peered inside. There was hummus and arugula and kale and not much else.

"People will be bringing sandwiches and watermelon," Mia offered.

"Hmmm." Violet was almost convinced. But then she opened the freezer. "Look! A frozen pizza! It's perfect."

"A frozen pizza?" Mia humphed. "You should still come.

Jay didn't want me to tell you, but he thinks you're really cute. Remember how you were this morning? Falling all over the place, forgetting your backpack, and stressed out? Guess he likes the frazzled, out-of-control type!"

Violet had too much on her mind to consider what she thought of Jay—if she liked the type who liked the frazzled, out-of-control type.

"I'm tempted," she told Mia. "And normally I'd go. I'd be thrilled to go! But I really need to get going on this script for TJ. I want it to be really good, and I'm going to have to work harder than I've ever worked before. I don't have much time to write."

She closed the freezer, the pizza box in hand. "Besides, this is sausage pizza! In a house full of health nuts. If I don't eat it, nobody will."

Violet sat in front of the laptop, the half-eaten pizza and a glass of water on her bedroom desk. She'd already chosen a font for the document and titled it *My Great Big Life-Changing Movie Script*. Now she stared at the blank screen.

A few minutes later, the screen still blank, she jumped up to put on her comfiest sweats. She always worked better when she felt relaxed.

She sat back down, cracking her knuckles to get the blood flowing.

Wait, she thought. *Now I'm too relaxed. I need to wake up!* She hurried downstairs to get an apple for dessert. She'd read somewhere that apples have as much caffeine as a cup of coffee. She didn't believe it, but it was true she always felt better after eating one.

Just in case it wasn't enough, she grabbed a carob bar, too. She would have preferred chocolate, but she had to take what she could get.

Now, this is better, she thought, back at the desk. She took a bite of the apple. "All set!" she said out loud.

Violet held her fingers poised over the keyboard. "All set!" she said again. Only she wasn't set. She didn't have a thought in her head, other than she really wanted a chocolate bar.

She spun around in her seat, finished the apple, and then polished off the cold pizza. When she turned back to the screen, it was blank. Surprise, surprise. She laughed at herself for half-hoping that, without any help from her, sentences would miraculously appear.

Just write anything to get started, Violet told herself. She typed in *anything*. Then she deleted it. She had to get to work, for real. She'd start with her main character from the first script—a sixteen-year-old girl named Melanie who'd just moved to a new town. She typed in a description: *Interior, Melanie's kitchen. She is putting a frozen pizza into the microwave.*

Boring, Violet thought. *And it certainly doesn't have heart.* Snickering, she added *spicy meatball with garlic and onion* to the pizza. "There," she said. "Now at least it will have heartburn!"

Sighing, Violet deleted each and every word. Then she noticed her fingernails. The polish had chipped off and they looked ragged. Immediately, she got a nail file and polish remover and went to work. Ten minutes passed, and finally, she was satisfied. Now, back to the script.

Violet turned to her laptop. She cracked her knuckles once again, ready to work. Hmmm. Maybe she should check her phone first and see if there were any texts. She wouldn't want to be distracted once she got in the groove. She swiped the screen.

Nothing.

She swiped it a few more times just to be sure texts hadn't come in right after she looked.

Still nothing.

Okay, back to work. For a few minutes, Violet stared at the screen, unmoving. The character Melanie was just plain boring. She needed inspiration. Maybe watching TV would help, give her some ideas for a new character or setting. She flopped on the bed, grabbed the remote, and started surfing through the channels.

First there was a reality show about the inner lives of cats . . . then reruns of old sitcoms . . . then news . . .

news . . . news . . . *Wait!* Violet went back to the last channel. It was a broadcast of *Hollywood This Week,* taped that morning and featuring none other than her own Hayes Grier.

Hayes was talking about Hawk and his character's girlfriend, Devon, with a sweet, serious expression, like their fate was the most important thing in the world.

Oh, he really was adorable. Violet was sure every girl watching imagined herself in Devon's shoes, racing through the woods hand in hand with Hawk/Hayes, running from the bad guys; not sure if her hammering heart was from exertion or from being so close to Hawk/Hayes.

Violet herself would face any sort of danger to be that girl. Then she had a sudden thought: Wouldn't it be amazing to write her own story about Hayes Grier and his love life? Something different, like a novel, so it wouldn't get in the way of her screenplay. A setting popped into her head. She could so see Hayes right there . . .

Without any hesitation, Violet flicked on the laptop and began to type.

> *The sun was rising, and Hayes Grier took in deep lungfuls of air.* Now this is living, *he thought.*
>
> *Hayes was hiking, alone, in LA's Griffith Park. He wanted some time away from his*

crazy Hollywood life. He loved every bit of the Hollywood scene—the insane schedules, his buddies, and the fun. But every once in a while he needed to be on his own to settle his head.

Of course, his loyal pup, Zan, was there, too. So Hayes wasn't really alone!

Hayes loved the calm and quiet of the shaded trail. He didn't pass one person. But just in case, he wore a baseball cap and shades. Hopefully, no one would recognize him. Hayes loved his fans, but sometimes it was good to get away from it all.

Suddenly, the silence was shattered. A girl was crying. Hayes hated to think of anyone in distress. So he followed the cries. "We have to help," he told Zan. Soon they arrived at the edge of the LA River.

Violet paused. Did the LA River even go through Griffith Park? Violet had been there plenty of times, hiking with Mia and her uncle, but they'd always gone straight up, climbing tough trails to the top of Beacon or Glendale Peak where all of LA spread before them, looking otherworldly in the smog. Did she have to be accurate in fan fiction? Probably not, she decided. She would just let her heart dictate what she wrote. Heart, that's what counted.

The water churned noisily, and Hayes spied a figure crouched by the river's edge. The figure stood. It was a girl about his own age, with long, curly red-brown hair . . .

Violet twirled a lock of her own curly hair.

. . . and big, glistening tears in her eyes. She really was in distress! Hayes rushed over, his hair flopping into his bright blue eyes. Of course he wanted to help. That was just the special kind of guy he was.

"What's wrong?" he asked, Zan at his heels. "Can I help?"

"Yes! Yes!" the girl answered. "My dog is trapped in the riverbed. I don't know what to do!"

She stretched out one arm. "I can't reach him."

Hayes looked out over the water and saw a dog's head popping up and down. He loved dogs—big ones, little ones, and all sizes in between. He couldn't bear to see one in trouble. "I see him!" he told her. "I can swim and get him.

"You stay here," he told Zan. "With—I don't even know your name."

"Rose."

"With Rose."

In a flash, he whipped off his cap and shades. He stripped off his T-shirt and dived in. He took long, sure strokes. "What's his name?" he called back to the girl.

"Fred!" she shouted.

He reached the dog and, treading water, cradled him against his chest. "Hi, Fred." The dog licked his face happily. "We're going back to shore."

With one arm, Hayes held the dog across his chest in a lifeguard carry and paddled back to shore.

"You saved Fred!" Rose jumped up and down. "How can I ever thank you?"

Hayes bowed. "Helping people is what I do," he told her, only half-joking. "And when I have the chance to help a cute girl and save a dog at the same time? It makes it even more satisfying."

Rose looked at him. "You seem awfully familiar," she said. "Do I know you from somewhere?"

Hayes grinned and . . .

Violet's fingers flew over the keys. She'd been having such a hard time writing before, but now the fanfic flowed.

She had a million ideas, each one better than the last, and the story just kept going and going.

Finally, Violet paused for a sip of water. She leaned back for a moment, taking a deep breath. How much had she written? She looked at the bottom of the screen for the count. Twenty-five pages! That was really unbelievable.

Violet typed a few more words, polishing the good-night kiss description. Then she yawned loudly.

Suddenly, she realized how tired she felt. The writing had been like a shot of caffeine with a chocolate bar chaser. If she hadn't stopped typing, she could have gone on forever; she'd never have noticed. But she did stop, and the crazy day had caught up to her. Still, more than anything, Violet wanted to keep going, keep writing.

She'd close her eyes for a minute, she decided. She'd take a little catnap, then get back to Hayes and the fanfic. She wouldn't even close her laptop. Smiling, she fell into bed, still in her clothes, and fell into a deep sleep.

"Knock, knock." Mia, just back from the beach, slowly opened Violet's bedroom door and peeked inside.

Violet snored gently, curled up like a kitten in bed. Careful not to wake her cousin, Mia pulled up the blanket and tucked it under Violet's chin. "There you go," she said softly. "Sweet dreams, Violet."

Mia backed away, accidentally nudging the laptop still open on the desk. The screen lit up.

"Oops!" Mia whispered. She went to close the top, but the words *Hayes Grier* made her stop. Were these notes for Violet's job? Maybe Mia could get an inside scoop right now. Maybe Violet hadn't told her everything!

Half-ashamed, half-excited, Mia read on.

"The sun was rising, and Hayes Grier took in big lungfuls of air," she read.

Violet hadn't been at the lot before sunrise today. This couldn't be real. It had to be made-up, a fan fiction–type story.

She shouldn't read it; Mia knew that. But Hayes Grier! Come on! Violet would understand. She'd surely do the same if their roles were reversed. They shared everything anyway. And assuming it was fan fiction, wasn't that what it was all about? Sharing?

Quietly, Mia sat down, scrolling through the pages, devouring every word.

Half an hour later, she was done. But Mia didn't want the story to end. She read the pages all over again. They were good; really good. The story deserved to have an audience—not just one sixteen-year-old girl, reading it alone in the middle of the night. She had to make it happen.

Mia googled fan-fiction sites. There were dozens, but she had to find just the right one. She read through description after description—mentally crossing off those that featured book or film characters. She clicked on sites, read entries on some, and then settled on one called Celeb Fan Tales.

Now she had to come up with a "handle," an alias for Violet so she could remain anonymous. Mia thought the whole world should know Violet Reeves wrote this piece. But just in case Violet wasn't thrilled with the idea, it seemed the best way to go.

HollywoodWriter310, she typed, then posted the story. *There*, she thought. It was clever to use the Venice area code in the handle, she thought. No one would ever have to know it was Violet.

CHAPTER FIVE

VIOLET'S PHONE ALARM sounded with a loud beep. She reached over sleepily and tried to turn it off, finally succeeding on the third attempt. Luckily, Violet had set the alarm riding home from work the day before. Oversleeping two mornings in a row would *not* be a good idea!

She closed her eyes again, trying to remember her dream. It was the kind of dream you want to continue. There was something about a dog and a river and Hayes Grier . . .

Violet smiled. It wasn't a dream; it was her story. She should really read it over. She'd typed so quickly, she'd probably made some typos. And she could probably strengthen the narrative; fiddle around with the wording. Not that it mattered! She giggled a bit. Nobody would ever see it. Still, she liked her writing to be as perfect as possible.

Violet flung off the blanket and stared at her legs. She was still wearing sweats? She ran her tongue over her teeth. They felt a little fuzzy, as if they were wearing mittens. She hadn't brushed them! It all came rushing back. The caffeine kick of writing. The sudden exhaustion. The thought that she'd just rest for a few minutes. Ha!

Violet rolled out of bed, eager to get into the shower.

But first, she had to go over the Hayes Grier story. She tapped her laptop, expecting the piece to materialize on-screen. Instead, she was looking at a website called Celeb Fan Tales. She scrolled down a bit and saw the title: "Hayes Grier Saves the Day!" What? Was that her story? It couldn't be. She wouldn't use that title; it sounded too much like a newspaper headline. She kept reading, and her stomach dropped, as if she were riding a crazy-fast roller coaster. It *was* her story. But how did it get on that site? There was only one answer.

"Mia!" she shouted. "Get in here right now!"

One second later, as if she were waiting outside the door, Mia waltzed in, calmly tying the belt on her kimono. "Yes?" she said sweetly.

"Did you read my Hayes story? And post it here?" Violet turned her laptop so Mia could see the screen.

"Oh, Violet!" Mia pulled her cousin onto the bed and held both her hands. "Don't be mad at me. Please!"

"Of course I'm mad!" Violet retorted. "How could you do something like this? I'm not sure I'd even let you read this, let alone send it out to the whole wide world!"

"I know," Mia said. "But I did read it. And I loved it! And I couldn't let it just sit there, doing nothing. I mean, these pages have so much heart—that's what you want in your writing. Right? I knew it would grab everyone's attention. Look!"

She stepped over to the desk, tapped a few keys on the computer, and swung the screen toward Violet. "See how many people read it already?"

Violet stood, going over to glance at the number. She blinked. Then she looked at it again: 228,622! More than two hundred thousand people! Five times the population of her hometown! She couldn't help but smile.

"See?" said Mia. "I did good, right?"

"Maybe," Violet admitted.

"Come on, definitely! You have a following, Violet! You, Violet Reeves, from Mills Landing, New York, have fans! And you deserve each and every one."

Violet flushed. Did she really?

"Now, shouldn't you say thank you?"

"Don't push it, Mia." Violet reached over and hugged her cousin tight. "Thanks, but you have to promise to never publish anything again without my permission."

Mia made an *X* over her chest. "Cross my heart. And to make it up to you right now? I think I'll whip up the specialty of the house, Eggs Venice, a work of art if I do say so myself—two poached eggs in a scooped-out avocado, on a bed of quinoa." She eyed the pizza plate. "I think you need some proper nourishment."

Mia left the room with a final hug, and Violet fell back on her pillow, grinning widely. When she really thought about it, being published on a fan-fiction site was kind of perfect. It made her feel successful, and writing, she knew, was all about confidence. *Anonymous fame*, she told herself. *What could be better?*

Her phone dinged with a text. It must be her mom, Violet figured. She'd barely spoken to her about the first day of work, and she probably wanted more information. Without looking, Violet started to tap on the contact details to make a FaceTime call but stopped short. The text wasn't from her mom. It was from Hayes. Now that would have been embarrassing! Not only would she have called him up, he'd have been able to see her rat's nest of hair and pizza crust teeth!

Hey, Violet read. *Just saying I'm sorry again. My crew is great. But sometimes when they're all together, they don't think about anything else but making each other laugh.* After she read it through—ten times!—Hayes sent a Snapchat, just to her. It was a picture of Hayes and Zan relaxing on the trailer couch, but their faces were swapped. Violet giggled wildly. Hayes was cute even when he had paws! *And* he was thinking of her, trying to get her to laugh. She sent back a laughing emoji, because really it was hilarious. And how nice of him to apologize—again!

"I can't even believe it," Violet said to his picture. "You're a supersweet guy."

Suddenly Violet sat up straight, her heart beating fast in panic. Hayes didn't want that hospital visit to be public news. For someone so out there on social media, he wanted certain parts of his life kept private. He wanted his actions to be real. And now she'd made up a whole parallel life for him. Her Hayes Grier fanfic was out there for everyone and anyone to see. What would he think about that?

Violet caught her breath.

He was a celebrity, an actor, a social media star. Not a writer. Hayes wouldn't understand about writer's block, how she couldn't come up with anything to write until she focused on him. How could she explain that once she started, she couldn't stop?

And after all that, she'd have to tell him she didn't post the story. Her cousin did. It all sounded like an out-and-out lie.

He'd hate the story. Hate her excuse. Worse, he'd hate her. And maybe just as bad, she'd lose her job and her chance at the recommendation letter for the Academy.

Violet had to keep it all secret. She had to keep the fan fiction from Hayes—no matter what!

PART TWO

Girl Likes Boy

CHAPTER SIX

"HEY, HAYES. SORRY TO KEEP YOU WAITING." TJ walked briskly into his World Famous office, pulled out a chair, and faced Hayes across the desk.

"Not a problem," said Hayes. He knew TJ was pulled in a thousand directions every day. The director was responsible for everything on set, and Hayes respected TJ's work ethic. He thought the guy was a little over the top, a little too out for himself, but maybe you had to be that way to be in charge of a huge cast and crew. So more power to him.

"What's up?"

TJ shuffled some papers, made a note on a pad, and

then swiveled in his chair, still not looking directly at Hayes. "There's been another change."

"Just as long as I don't have to weep uncontrollably all through the movie, it's all good," Hayes joked.

TJ smiled distractedly. "No, nothing like that. In fact, it's something that will actually make your life easier."

"Sounds good." Hayes waited expectantly.

"I'm pulling you from the motorcycle stunt."

"What? You're cutting the scene where Hawk rides around speeding cars on the LA freeway, dodging the bad guys?"

"Why would we cut that?" TJ barked out a laugh. "That's the best chase scene we have. It's pivotal."

"So what gives?"

"I'm having a professional stuntman do the scene. It's too dangerous. We need you to survive filming. Don't forget, you have to promote the movie after it wraps."

Hayes eyed him. TJ was talking in a jokey, guy-to-guy way, but Hayes knew he was dead serious. Hayes was serious, too, though—serious about doing his own stunts, and serious about riding that motorcycle. It would be a total blast, and he grew up riding motorbikes, so he knew what he was doing.

"Listen, I've been practicing every day," Hayes said. "And it's all on set. The whole thing is choreographed. It's safer than my commute to the studio!"

"You do have a history," TJ reminded him.

"One little accident on a dirt bike!"

"You were in the hospital for days."

"Yeah, but I never want to go through that again! The boredom alone could have killed me. Trust me, TJ, I learned from that accident. I can do these stunts."

TJ stood. "My mind is made up." He headed toward the door. "Concentrate on acting, Hayes, not biking, and don't try to convince me otherwise. My decision is final."

Alone in TJ's office, Hayes slumped in his chair. He knew he could handle the stunt. If they had to take something away, why couldn't it be that big emotional scene? Why couldn't TJ get a stuntman for that?

Violet was in wardrobe, picking up a pair of tattered jeans for Hayes. The pants looked like a truck had run them over, but that was probably the point, she figured. "Thanks, Tess," she said to the assistant, then headed outside.

"Violet!" TJ hurried over. "I need your help."

Violet grinned. Anything she could do for TJ would only help her chances at getting that letter. "Sure," she said.

"It's simple," TJ told her. "Just keep Hayes off motorcycles. He's not doing any stunts in the movie, and I don't want him riding one at all. I want him in one piece."

Of course you do, Violet said to herself. *Hayes is the star of the movie.* Her only question was, why did TJ say Hayes could ride the bike in the first place? Maybe he'd finally realized it could be dangerous, especially since Hayes liked speed. Whatever; she wasn't going to get on his case about that now.

TJ must have caught her expression. "What, you have a problem?"

"No!"

"Then just keep him off that bike. If I catch him riding, you can forget your script and your recommendation. Got it?"

"Got it," Violet repeated. "And I promise you will not see Hayes on a motorcycle."

TJ hurried away, flipping through his clipboard, muttering to himself, already on to the next problem.

Violet shifted the jeans to the other arm. Maybe this would be a simple assignment. Maybe Hayes wanted to stay safe, too. Maybe riding a motorcycle was the last thing on his mind.

She could always hope.

Violet's phone buzzed with another text from Hayes. He must have sent her a dozen already, asking her to run an errand, giving her an update on his plans, or just making a silly comment. Each time, her heart skipped a beat. Hayes Grier was texting *her*!

Could you meet me in the trailer in 20? Violet read. *To run lines?*

Violet grinned. Running lines was definitely going to be her favorite part of the job. Sitting with Hayes, reading over the script, and kind-of-sort-of acting right along with him. Quickly she answered with a thumbs-up emoji.

Holding the phone, Violet couldn't resist texting Mia: *About to run lines with H! Hope I can pull it off!* But this was the last time she'd fill Mia in on her Hayes duties—it wasn't the most professional thing to do. And Violet had to take this job superseriously.

Violet checked the time. She didn't want to get to Hayes's trailer too early. Still holding the jeans, she wandered around the lot, skirting a fake laboratory soundstage. Production assistants were setting up all sorts of high-tech-looking equipment and computers along shiny metal lab tables.

She kept walking, and across the lot, she saw assistant directors testing camera angles for a school cafeteria scene. "Devon will stand right here," one said, waving to a stand-in who looked like a high school student. The actress—the real Devon—sat in a director's chair, watching.

"Coco!" the assistant director called out. "This is going to take a while. You can break for a bite to eat."

So this is the famous Coco, Violet thought. *Hayes's costar.* The actress had long, straight black hair tucked behind her ears, and was dressed in short-shorts and a tank top, a regular type of outfit, cute but not very revealing. Was that how she normally dressed? Violet wondered. Or was that in character?

Violet had known, of course, that Coco was in the movie, too. Everyone knew sixteen-year-old Coco—just Coco. No last name. She'd been a child star, playing a lead role in the nighttime soap *Family Album*, about a dad and his kids forming a band.

Coco had never gone through an awkward phase or needed braces. She'd never been photographed looking less than perfect. She sailed effortlessly through adolescence into teen stardom, and now was Hollywood's latest "it" girl—the actress every director wanted in his movie.

Coco walked to the craft service tables, going in the same direction as Violet. She paused in front of one table, and Violet slowed, too—almost as fascinated to see her in person as she had been to see Hayes.

Coco bent to look over a cookie tray. "Oh!" she gasped, so loudly everyone stopped what they were doing. Quickly, she spun away from the table with a look of panicked horror.

She placed one hand on her stomach, the other on her chest, and took dramatic deep, slow breaths, trying to calm down as everyone looked on. With one last noisy breath, she grabbed a production assistant by the arm. "Listen," she said harshly. "There are peanut butter cookies on that table. I won't stand for that!"

Violet snorted. What, they didn't have Coco's favorite

cookie? She seemed to recall it was mocha-mint macarons. Typical bratty child star behavior. *I'd hate to be her assistant!* Violet thought. If Hayes didn't like a certain cookie, he'd just say, no thanks.

"Oh, hey!" Violet, lost in thought, hadn't realized Coco was standing in front of her.

"I'm Coco," the actress said, seeming to forget all about the cookie incident. "I haven't seen you on set before."

"I'm Violet, Hayes's assistant," Violet explained. "I just started yesterday."

"How do you like it so far?"

Coco sounded friendly. But what if Violet said or did something to annoy her? She'd probably have to start those breathing exercises all over again. "It's been good," she answered cautiously, taking a step back.

Coco stepped forward. "Are you from LA?"

"Um, no." Why was Coco being so chatty? It almost seemed like she wanted to be friends.

"Wait, let me try and guess by your accent."

Accent? Violet didn't even know she had an accent!

"Western Massachusetts?"

"That's not too far off," Violet conceded as she backed farther away. "Upstate New York. Listen, I've got to go."

"Oh, that's too bad." Coco sounded genuinely disappointed. "I hope I see you around. Maybe we can grab something to eat outside the lot sometime." Once again, she edged closer to Violet, who noticed her hazel eyes. "I hate to say anything bad about anyone, but I don't really trust some of these production assistants or craft service people. Did you see what just happened?"

Violet nodded, curious to see how Coco would explain away her tantrum.

"Well, I have a severe peanut allergy. And TJ told the whole crew about it. He said no peanuts in any food. And right there, mixed in with the chocolate chip and fudge and vanilla cookies, were peanut ones. And they looked just like the vanilla cookies! If I'd taken one bite, I would have had a reaction and could have stopped production for days."

"Oh!" Strangely enough, Violet had never read that Coco had any allergies. "It's funny I didn't know that," she told Coco. "The tabloids put out so much information on you."

Coco humphed. "Wrong information you mean! They never get anything straight. Half the time they make me out to be some sort of spoiled diva."

Violet flushed. That was exactly what she'd thought.

"I bet if I ended up in the hospital because of that cookie and missed shooting, it would be all over the news. But they wouldn't mention the allergy. They'd just jump to some crazy conclusion and put me in the center of a scandal. They'd say I'm refusing to go to work, heartbroken because Hayes didn't want to date me. Or I'm having a fling with a married actor and have run off to a tropical island."

Violet wasn't quite sure what to say. Should she address the media gossip or the peanut allergy? "It's good that you're watching out for yourself," she said, trying to cover both.

"Exactly!" Coco beamed. "Health is the most important thing there is."

Just then Violet's phone sounded. "Oh!" she said. "I forgot about running lines! It must be Hayes. I'm supposed to be in his trailer right now!"

"I'll walk you." Coco linked arms with Violet as they moved across the lot. "You know," she confided, "I grew up in the industry. And I was always close with my TV family. But nobody was my age. And I really would love a girlfriend. It would be totally great just to have a regular type of friendship."

Violet smiled. She'd been way off base about Coco. She seemed really nice. And it would be good to have someone else to hang around with besides Mia. "I'd like that, too," she told Coco.

Just as Violet approached Hayes's trailer a few minutes later, the door swung open. "I've been waiting for you!" Hayes said, beckoning her inside.

Uh-oh. She must be late. She'd lost track of time talking with Coco. Hayes didn't seem like he'd be a stickler for punctuality but you never knew. Maybe TJ was rubbing off on him.

"I'm so sorry!" Violet rushed inside, placed his jeans on the dresser, and reached for her own copy of the script. "Let's start quickly then."

Zan bounded over, wagging his tail happily. One of Violet's duties was to walk Zan when Hayes wasn't around, and the two had developed a connection. She leaned down, scratching him behind the ear.

"No, no, it's okay. We don't have to rush." Hayes walked right past his own script to kneel next to Zan and scratch his other ear. Zan, in heaven, thumped his tail loudly on the floor.

Violet's and Hayes's fingers were so close, if Violet moved her pinky a quarter of an inch, they'd be touching. Their eyes met over Zan's head, and for a moment Violet forgot where she was and what she was supposed to be doing.

"I guess I just wanted someone to talk to," Hayes admitted, leaning back.

The spell was broken.

"Why?" Violet managed to say.

Hayes frowned. "TJ just told me I can't do my own motorcycle stunts. I'm pissed; it really stinks."

"That's too bad," Violet said carefully. She couldn't lose sight of her own assignment: keeping Hayes off that bike.

"But let's talk about something else." Hayes took Violet's

script out of her hand and put it on the table. "It will take my mind off everything here and help me focus later."

"Okay," Violet said slowly. "What do you want to talk about?" She bit her lip. She probably sounded like some sort of therapist.

Hayes shrugged. "Whatever. Why don't you start? Tell me about your family."

Violet told him about her parents back east, Mia, and Uncle Forrest.

"So you're far from home, too," Hayes said sympathetically. "Sometimes it makes me sad that I'm here, and my family isn't." He busied himself pouring two strawberry smoothies from a pitcher, and Violet sensed he didn't want to meet her eyes while he talked about his feelings.

Hayes carried over the drinks, then sat next to Violet on the couch.

"I mean, I love the entertainment industry. But every once in a while it hits me that I haven't seen my family in ages."

"That must be tough," Violet agreed.

"And LA is great and everything, but back home I'm outdoors practically 24/7, on my family's ranch. Thank God for Zan here. Otherwise, I'd hardly see any animals at all. On the ranch, there are all these different animals just hanging around, and there's always something that needs to be done to take care of them."

Hayes leaned closer to Violet now, finally gazing right at her. "Nobody knows this, but one time I even swam with a horse, crossing this major river. His name was Dallas, and I'll never forget it. But stuff like that isn't easy to do around here."

Hayes looked at her even more intently. Violet felt her face grow hot. She had to get past this celebrity crush feeling. Hayes was a real person.

"But that sounds like I'm not grateful for everything I have here. And that's not true at all! That would be crazy!"

"But you can't help how you feel," Violet put in. "I'm kind of in the same boat. I'm here in LA, and have this amazing opportunity on set, to learn all about movies . . . I want to write screenplays . . . but I keep thinking about this one ice-cream place back home and how my parents and I walk there almost every night after dinner. I always see someone I know, a friend from school or just someone from the neighborhood, and we usually wind up doing something afterward. I miss home," Violet said softly. Now she was the one not meeting Hayes's eyes. "My parents have been great about all this. They really want to support me. But I miss them. I miss my friends. I miss that ice cream. I even miss my mom pulling off my blanket in the morning to wake me up. LA is so different. I really miss looking at the sky at night and seeing stars. Here . . ." she trailed off, shrugging.

"It's hard to see the stars through all that smog," Hayes finished for her.

"Exactly! And without the stars, I lose something. I don't know . . . I don't have that sense of connection with the universe." Violet gave a half-laugh, embarrassed to be talking like that. But Hayes gave an understanding nod. So she kept going.

"You know, the peacefulness of knowing you're not alone and that the universe, so breathtakingly beautiful, goes on forever. And you get the sense that anything can happen because there's just so much . . . so much life . . . out there."

Oh God, she really went too far. But this was something she felt deeply about, staring at the stars, thinking she *could* write. She had the potential, she just had to reach for the stars and believe it. And she had an idea that Hayes would understand it all—the homesickness, the longing.

Finally, she lifted her eyes. Hayes was gazing at her with such compassion, she reached out her hand toward him. He moved closer and—

Bang! The door swung open with a crash and Tez flung himself inside. "Shove over," he said to Hayes, plopping down between the two.

Violet shrank back, remembering yesterday's embarrassment. Tez nodded at her briefly but thankfully didn't bring up that crazy "I love you" or walking into walls.

"Just brought over your motorcycle, bro," he told Hayes. "Got the engine checked. Now she's riding like a dream."

Hayes scowled. "Well, you're going to have to ride it right back out of here. TJ just ordered me to stay away from bikes."

Violet breathed a sigh of relief. Hayes understood. He was going to listen to TJ without any involvement from her. That made it all so much easier.

"What do you mean?" Tez cried. "How are you going to do the big chase scene? On a tricycle?"

"That's off. I mean, I'm off. The stunt goes on without me."

"That's whack." Tez jumped up as if he were going to run right over to TJ and tell him what he thought.

"I know." Hayes sounded miserable. "But what can I do?"

"Well, nothing, I guess."

Yes! Violet gave a little fist pump, so small a movement, no one could even notice.

"Nothing as far as the movie goes," Tez went on. "But you also have a whole other life, and you can do what you want. Besides, you've been practicing like crazy. You know what you're doing on that scooter."

Uh-oh. Tez was taking it in the wrong direction now.

"You told me you just mastered the sickest wheelie of all time, man—the cliff-hanger!"

Violet groaned quietly. That definitely didn't sound good. If Tez kept talking like that, she'd have to build up her courage and say something.

"And you haven't even shown it to me." Tez paced back and forth. "Come on, Grier! Show me right now."

"Ahem." Violet blushed. She sounded like her old chemistry teacher. But she plowed ahead, saying, "Hayes, that's not a good idea. TJ knows what he's doing. If he doesn't want you on that bike, you shouldn't get on it."

There, she spoke up. Hayes turned to her and smiled. "I won't get on," he told her.

She smiled back.

"After today," he finished. "I just want to show Tez these moves, and then he'll drive it off the lot. I swear I won't ride again until after filming. No one will see me; no one will know."

Be assertive, Violet told herself. *Put your foot down. Come right out and say he can't ride at all.*

"Hayes," she began.

But then her phone beeped, then beeped again and again, vibrating noisily in her bag. "One sec," she said, pausing to check it.

Message after message filled the screen. At first, she didn't understand. Who were all these people trying to get in touch with her? Hayesluvr. Vinestarfollower. Griergirl?

Then she read more carefully.

Crazy about ur story, said one message. *Write more—quickly!* said another. *Luv ur FF.*

Then it hit her. These were messages from the fanfic site. Mia must have linked her phone. *Please, please, please!* read the next. *You have to give us more Hayes. When's the next story? WHAT HAPPENS NEXT?*

Violet scrolled through each one, her heart racing. People were begging HollywoodWriter310 to keep going. They liked her writing! The reviews were glowing!

A loud revving sound suddenly filled the trailer. "Hayes?" she said, finally pulling her eyes from the phone. "What's going on?"

"Hayes?" She did a quick 360 around the room, then checked the rest of the trailer, searching for Hayes. It was empty. He and Tez had left without her even realizing it.

Outside, an engine gunned again. Not just any engine. A motorcycle. Her heart pounding, she raced out the door.

She had to stop Hayes.

Violet thought quickly. Tez said he'd parked the bike in the back. She raced around the trailer. The engine's roar sounded again.

"Hayes!" she shouted. She turned the corner in time to see a stream of exhaust fade into nothingness. Hayes was gone, along with Tez and the motorcycle.

Violet took off in the direction of the exhaust, listening intently for the sound of a motorcycle. She heard a truck backfire, but that was all. Still, she kept running. Twenty minutes later, she realized it was a lost cause. Hayes was nowhere to be found.

Violet closed her eyes in frustration. She'd totally messed up. She and Hayes hadn't gone over the lines as planned. But that was nothing compared to this, a mistake so big, she could barely believe she'd made it.

Violet had let Hayes ride off on a motorcycle. Not just ride, she corrected herself. She'd let him leave to do a . . . to do a . . . what was it? A cliff-hanger!

Violet caught her breath, finally slowing down. She stopped by the craft service table to grab a bottled water.

"You look like you've just had a major workout. Been rushing around the set looking for something?" TJ asked. Violet's eyes snapped wide open.

"Wait." TJ stopped short. "You didn't really lose him, did you? Where is Hayes?"

Violet bit her lip. What could she possibly say?

CHAPTER SEVEN

A LITTLE WHILE LATER, Violet sat in TJ's office, anxiously waiting to talk to him. Her stomach clenched with apprehension; she felt like she'd been called to the principal's office and was about to get a talking-to. Not that Violet knew what that felt like. She'd never been in trouble at school, not once in eleven years. But now, after only two days on the job, she'd messed up big time.

Luckily, after TJ had asked where Hayes was, he'd been called away before she could answer; something about some props being sent to Hollywood, Florida, not Hollywood, California. As he raced away, he'd shouted over his shoulder that he wanted her to go to his office—"Now!"—and stay there until he finished putting out the latest fire.

But Violet still had no idea what to tell him. She wanted to blurt out the truth. To tell him Hayes had ridden off on the motorcycle and she'd barely tried to stop him. But she knew it would be professional suicide. She wanted to go to the Academy more than anything. She *needed* to go to the Academy. It was her lifelong dream. Everyone back home knew about it . . . everyone here knew about it, too. Her parents had helped her get to this point, paying for her writing classes, driving her to every movie she wanted to see. It would be too hard to tell them; to tell anyone.

Besides, she didn't want to tell on Hayes. She couldn't bear for him to get in trouble, either.

"So," TJ said, walking in, not even saying hello. "Is there any kind of problem?"

"Problem?" Violet repeated, stalling for time.

"Yes, where is Hayes?" TJ sounded so impatient, she couldn't put him off any longer.

She would make something up. It would be okay. She wouldn't be fired. And Hayes would be fine, too. Like he'd said, it was just this one time. No one would ever have to know.

Thinking quickly now, she told TJ, "He's working on his lines for that high school cafeteria scene, where he sneaks back to school to talk to Devon."

TJ raised one eyebrow. "Where exactly? Is he still on the lot?"

Now Violet's words came quickly. It was almost like writing the fanfic, all the right words popping into her brain at once.

"He's kind of in seclusion . . . I don't even know where . . . doing some sense memory work. He wants to really get into his character, you know, to get that feeling of being in a high school cafeteria. He said something about concentrating on day-old meatloaf."

"Hmmm, that sounds good." TJ nodded. "I'm guessing that was your idea, Violet. Very impressive."

Violet was about to set him straight on that at least. But then she heard the roar of a motorcycle, coming just outside the office. She froze, her back to the window. She didn't turn around, but the sound grew louder, and she saw TJ's expression as his eyes moved from left to right, following, no doubt, the motorcycle's path.

He rushed to the window and banged on it—as if that would bring Hayes back. Then he glared at Violet, his face bright red with anger. "Violet!" he fumed. "I told you to keep Hayes off that thing, in no uncertain terms. And you agreed. And now you're lying to me? Making up some silly story about acting techniques so I wouldn't send someone looking for him?"

Violet stood up, too. This was awful, horrible. Why did she think lying solved anything? Of course she'd told little white lies before. "No, you don't look fat." "Yes, dinner was delicious." But this was an all-time whopper, *and* she'd been caught.

TJ would kick her off the set. He'd tell everyone what happened. She'd never get a job in Hollywood—or anywhere else—ever.

"I'm so sorry, TJ. I don't know why I lied. It's not like me at all—really." She couldn't stop babbling. How would she explain this to her parents? To Mia and her uncle? And to Hayes? "I'll get my things and leave the lot."

TJ sat back heavily in his chair. He rubbed his temples, sighing loudly. "I'm not firing you, Violet. At least not yet. I don't have anyone to replace you." He looked straight at her, his eyes softening a bit.

"And I can understand why you did it. Almost. But I need to be able to trust you. Hayes is the most important part of this production—not counting me, of course—and nothing can happen to him."

"You can trust me!" Violet stood up straighter.

"Okay," TJ said. "I'm giving you one more chance." He almost smiled at her. "How many chances, Violet?"

"One!" Violet held up her pointer finger.

"That's right, one. And don't forget it. Because if anything else goes wrong, then you really are out of here. You can kiss that recommendation letter good-bye, too. I wouldn't read that new script—ever."

"Right," she agreed.

"Now get out of here."

Without another word, Violet tiptoed past TJ and into the hall. That meeting was more difficult than anything she'd had to deal with before. It was way worse than the combination parent-teacher-student conference in sixth grade, when her teacher—insisting on open communication at all levels—told her parents she had a crush on Timmy Gould.

Now she had to talk to Hayes; tell him that TJ had found out about the bike. And she felt more nervous than when she'd asked little Timmy if she could borrow his pencil.

Violet reached the trailer just as Tez took off on the motorcycle. Inside, Hayes was eating cereal over the sink. Zan circled his feet, hoping some Sugar Crunchies would fall on the floor.

This is good, Violet thought. *We're alone. Hayes and I can talk things through.*

Hayes grinned at her, still excited about the ride. "You should have seen me, Violet! I did a perfect cliff-hanger! Then I took her out one last time. I just had to. But see? Everything worked out fine. I'm here, safe and sound, and Tez and the motorcycle are gone."

"Everything did not work out fine." Violet settled into a

comfy chair clear across the room. She wanted to keep as much distance as she could between them. If she got too close to Hayes, she doubted she'd be able to sound firm and professional. That fangirl crush was still going strong, even though Hayes was turning out to be a regular guy.

"What do you mean?"

"I just came from TJ's office. You rode right past his window. He saw you."

"He did?" He put his head in his hands. "God, Violet, I wasn't even thinking!"

"Well, you should start now," she told him seriously. "I asked you to stay off the bike. But the request really came from TJ. Not me. It wasn't cool that you rode off, not listening. TJ was really angry. It put my internship—and basically the rest of my working life—on the line. I could have lost my job and TJ could have bad-mouthed me all over Hollywood. I'd be washed up at sixteen."

Hayes looked at her, astonished, and almost dropped the cereal bowl. Milk sloshed over the edges, dripping onto his black V-necked T-shirt.

"You're kidding. I had no idea how serious this is for you. I just wanted to have fun. I really wasn't thinking, Violet, I'm really sorry." He sounded so distraught, Violet—already emotional—felt like she might cry. She sniffled.

Hayes put the bowl down, then crossed the room to sit on the arm of her chair. Zan followed. "Really, V. I feel terrible. Can you forgive me?" He reached over to pluck a tissue from the box on the coffee table.

"Of course I can." Violet took the tissue and dabbed her nose. "Nobody's perfect. Certainly not me," she added to herself.

"From here on in, when you say 'jump,' I say 'how high,'" Hayes promised.

"Well, I'm not sure that's totally necessary." Violet laughed, then found herself almost crying again.

"Seriously, I didn't mean to disrespect you. I'll do whatever you say."

"Okay," Violet agreed. "You can start by getting over to the set. You're wanted in five."

Hayes leaped to his feet and gave a mock salute. Then he was gone.

Violet stood slowly, picking up the bowl and putting it in the dishwasher—one of her assistant duties was keeping the trailer neat. She was tidying up a bit more when her phone buzzed. *Just wanted you to know I'm here on set,* Hayes texted. *Right on time.*

Violet grinned. He really was a good guy.

That afternoon, Violet rushed over to the cafeteria set, carefully carrying a coconut-almond cappuccino—plus a fruit cup!—for TJ. He'd texted her the request, and how could she say no? She wanted to do everything right, and running errands for the director was still apparently part of her internship.

Besides, now she had an excuse to watch some filming, and not just run from wardrobe to dry cleaning to Hayes's trailer.

Hayes and Coco stood off to the side, going over lines together from one script, their heads close together. On the set itself, "students" sat at tables, most just talking and waiting, surrounded by fake sandwiches and real water bottles.

Violet's gaze swung back to Hayes and Coco. They looked pretty cozy together. If Violet had run those lines with Hayes like she was supposed to, they would probably be across the room from each other, not side by side.

"Okay, everyone!" the assistant director called through a megaphone. "We're going to start. Hayes! Coco! Hit your marks. Quiet on the set!"

Coco slid into a chair at a table packed with good-looking guys and two other girls. She was dressed the same way she'd been earlier—in a tank and shorts. But now she looked tired. A makeup artist had applied powder to give her dark circles under her eyes, and her hair was disheveled.

Hayes walked to the cafeteria entrance, flipping his hood up and straightening his tattered jeans.

Another assistant held the clapperboard in front of the

camera. "Scene 26, Take 1," she announced, snapping the board closed.

The camera guys swung around to get the right angle. The focus was on Hayes, who was carefully arranging his features—from an anxious look to a deliberately laid-back one.

"Action!" called TJ.

Students talked quietly for background noise, the murmur of a busy high school cafeteria filled the air. Hayes sauntered over to Coco's table. When he drew close, the guys and girls stopped talking and stared at him.

"Hawk!" Coco jumped to her feet. "You're back in school! Where have you been? I've been calling and texting for two days. Your parents have been going crazy looking for you."

Hayes pulled her off to the side. The camera rolled closer, and the other actors quietly melted away. Coco stood with her back to the wall. Hayes faced her, standing close. He placed his arms on either side of her, hands pressing against the wall as if he wanted to hold her in place, to keep her close to him.

Coco tilted her head so their noses touched. She drew back slowly while Hayes bent closer. He was whispering and she was answering softly, but their words didn't really matter, Violet thought. The chemistry alone could carry the scene.

Violet sucked in her breath, a mix of feelings traveling down to her toes. Excitement: The movie was going to be the biggest smash of the summer. Envy: Coco and Hayes would surely be linked now, together forever in a way that couldn't be matched—at least not by a lowly intern running around getting coffee and picking up dry cleaning.

Violet pushed the thought away. What was she doing, comparing herself to Coco and an on-screen made-up relationship? She and Hayes had shared one sweet moment of connection and dozens of trivial conversations centered on schedules or food orders. Did that really amount to anything? And did she even want it to?

When it came down to it, did she have a fangirl crush, or something more?

"Cut!" shouted TJ. "Let's try the scene from the top again, but we need to figure out a different camera angle. You two"—he waved at Hayes and Coco—"take a break."

Together, Hayes and Coco walked away, their heads still close together. They went to a table in a quiet out-of-the-way spot. Hayes picked up his phone and showed Coco something on-screen. They both laughed.

Violet should be asking Hayes right now if he needed anything; some water, a snack. Instead, she hung back. Maybe they were staying in character, keeping up the boyfriend/girlfriend vibe. If that was the case, she didn't want to get in their way. But maybe, she thought with a pang, this was real. Maybe something was really going on between them. She watched Coco giggle and look up at Hayes, her head tilted adorably. Were they flirting? And could she really be jealous? She didn't know what to think.

So stop thinking! Violet told herself. *Remember, no thoughts on romance this summer. Concentrate on your job.*

For the rest of the afternoon, Violet hung around on set, helping the production assistants and going on coffee runs. She and Hayes exchanged smiles and a few words here and there, but they were both busy, and Violet felt relieved those crazy-weird feelings had just about passed.

"Okay, everyone!" TJ announced around four p.m. "That's it for the day."

The cast and crew talked a bit, then shuffled away.

"Violet!" TJ approached in his hurried, distracted way, thrusting out some papers. "Here's the schedule for tomorrow, and some notes on the next scene for Hayes. Make sure you go over every little thing with him, right now. We ran late today, and I want to make sure everything goes smoothly tomorrow."

"Of course!" Violet said brightly. But she was talking to herself. TJ had already spun on his heels and stalked away.

Violet found Hayes in the corner, pulling the hoodie over his head. "Hey!" she said.

"Hey!" he answered, smiling. He tossed the hoodie on a table and grinned. "That really needs to be washed."

Violet's heart sank. Taking care of his wardrobe was part of her job. So why did Hayes's saying that make her feel bad?

"Of course," she said in a businesslike way, scooping up the sweatshirt. "I'll get right on it."

"Violet." Hayes touched her arm. "I didn't mean it like that. I was just making a comment. It's really hot under those lights, and I've been wearing that sweatshirt all day."

Immediately, Violet's mood shifted. "Oh, okay. But I'll still take care of it. And we should really go over your schedule for tomorrow."

"I know." Hayes sighed. "What time is it?"

Violet glanced at her phone. "4:10."

"I hate to do this, V, but can we do it first thing in the morning? I have a meeting with my team now. Stu has to get to the airport to catch a flight to New York, and I don't want to make him late." He paused. "I'd love to stay here with you, but I've got to get going."

"Go, go!" Violet playfully pushed him away. She understood, and she liked that he didn't want to cause problems for Stu. "But we really have to get together at some point."

She watched Hayes turn to leave, thinking, *He said he'd love to stay with me!* Her heart beat fast. *Would he say that to Coco, too?*

"I'll text with your call time!" she shouted after him, a smile in her voice.

Hayes nodded and waved, but the second he turned the corner and was out of sight, worry set in. TJ had explicitly told her to meet with Hayes.

What if tomorrow morning they didn't connect? What if she missed him and couldn't tell him everything he needed to know? If there were any problems, she'd be in trouble. Again.

And this time, she'd be flat out of chances.

CHAPTER EIGHT

"MIA? WHERE ARE YOU?"

Violet walked into the house after work, feeling the need to see a friendly face, someone who already thought she was competent and hardworking.

"Up here!" Mia called. "In my room."

Violet walked up the steps to Mia's bedroom, her feet dragging. Inside, Mia sat on the floor, swatches of fabric spread around her. She held up her sketchbook, opened to a rough pencil drawing of a funky, long, flowing dress—a cross between a wedding gown and her kimono. "It's still a work in progress. I'm hoping if I find the right fabric, the rest will fall into place."

"It's looking good," Violet said. It was, but her voice came out scratchy and flat.

Mia looked at her more closely. "What's wrong?"

"Just a tough day on set." For some reason, Violet didn't want to go into the whole story—about Hayes and Coco and how she might have messed up again.

"Well, I'll show you something that will cheer you right up." Mia jumped to her feet, and opened a screen on her computer.

It was Violet's fanfic page—with hundreds more comments and thousands more reads. "Can you believe it?" Mia asked, her voice rising with excitement. "Your fanfic is breaking records. It's the hottest thing around."

"It's the featured story of the site?" Violet grinned.

"Yeah, so it will get even more hits. It's all over the fanfic stratosphere!"

"This is so weird." Violet shook her head. People were actually talking about her writing. They liked it!

She flopped onto Mia's bed to think, letting her cousin get back to her design. A million thoughts ran through her head . . . Hayes . . . Coco . . . TJ . . . And what about the fan fiction?

Violet scrolled through her website messages, reading more comments. Clearly, people wanted her to keep going, to add more to the story. She hadn't really thought about continuing—or even putting it out there to begin with!

(Thanks, Mia.) But it *was* out there. She couldn't take it back. And maybe she wouldn't want to anyway.

It was anonymous. No one knew the writer was Violet Reeves, wannabe screenwriter. And any writing teacher would say it was important to keep writing, no matter what. If you were blocked in one form, try another.

Readers didn't know she was Hayes Grier's assistant, and had an up-close glimpse into his life. So it wasn't really an invasion of privacy—right?

Right, she told herself.

So it wouldn't hurt to add a bit more . . . see how a relationship between Hayes Grier and a regular girl—like Violet—would play out in "real life." She went into her room and turned on the laptop . . .

> . . . *The whole school buzzed with excitement. Prom was in just a few weeks, and it was all anyone could talk about. Who was going with whom? What was everyone wearing?*
>
> *And how great was the theme, people crowed. The '90s! The decade of the original* Full House! *And those adorable Beanie Babies stuffed animals!*

Luckily Violet had watched a lot of movies from the '90s. She was almost an expert.

Back then, everyone dressed like they were part of a grunge band in flannel shirts and torn jeans. Should prom-goers incorporate that look into tuxes and long gowns? Should they practice the Macarena? There was going to be a dance contest, too, with one lucky couple winning a day at the amusement park at Santa Monica Pier.

Yes, everyone was talking about prom. And the biggest question on everyone's lips: Who would Hayes Grier go with? The night was fast approaching, and Hayes hadn't made his move. Plenty of girls had turned down dates, hoping Hayes would ask them, hoping they'd be the ones to slow dance with him to romantic songs by Mariah Carey.

Then, finally, word got out. Today was the day that Hayes would ask a girl. Each time he walked into class, the room fell silent.

Will he ask someone now? people wondered. In history? In bio? In Healthy Cooking/Healthy Eating?

Crowds parted to let him through the halls, eyes watching his every move. When he stopped, everyone held their breath. When he kept going, they sighed.

"Hi, Hayes," girls cried after him. "Hayes! How are you?"

Just after the bell, Hayes walked past a row of lockers. Everyone peered over their shoulders as he passed. Finally, he slowed, then paused. "Hi, Rose," he said.

"It's the new girl," someone whispered. "The one with that dog who jumped into the river."

People edged closer, unable to resist watching.

"How's Fred doing?"

"He's fine," Rose answered, her face turning a pretty shade of pink. Rose was too new to be in on the school gossip. But even she knew what this meant. The guy every girl wanted for her date was going to ask her to prom. Her!

Hayes reached into his backpack, slung casually over one shoulder, and drew out a single perfect red rose. "I saw this and thought of you," he said. "And I thought it would be the perfect way to ask: Will you go to prom with me?"

Feeling faint, Rose leaned against her locker. But the door was open, and she fell back. Quickly, Hayes reached to steady her and kept his arm around her shoulder.

"Yes," she whispered. "Yes, I'll go."

The hall erupted. Boys cheered. Girls groaned with disappointment. Hayes Grier was taken.

At prom, Hayes and Rose spent every minute together. They talked quietly by the drinks; they went from table to table, saying hello to friends. Then they moved to the dance floor, jumping and bouncing to a series of hard-rocking songs. Then, finally, the band played a ballad. They melted against each other. They swayed back and forth, barely moving.

"This night has been perfect," Hayes murmured in her ear. "And the most perfect part is being here with you."

The prom lights dimmed and . . .

Violet straightened with a start, her writing interrupted by wind chimes, doubling as a doorbell. She glanced at the time. It was after seven. She'd been writing for hours.

Then her door creaked open. "Violet?" Mia poked her head in, trying to hold back a grin but not quite succeeding. For one irrational moment, Violet thought Hayes had come to the house.

Mia swung the door open wider, and Jay walked into the room.

Violet quickly closed the laptop screen. "You're here to see me?" Violet said, surprised. Mia stepped away, leaving Jay standing alone.

"I hope this isn't a bad time . . . I know it's kind of late . . ." he trailed off uncertainly, and Violet hoped she hadn't sounded rude.

"No, it's fine," she assured him. "I'm just catching up on some . . . on some writing."

"Mia told me you want to be a screenwriter. It's cool that you're so into it."

"Well, everyone needs a hobby, right?" Violet said lightly. With her writing career in a precarious state, she didn't want anyone to know just how serious she was.

"Sure."

Jay looked cute, shuffling his feet a little awkwardly, wearing skinny, checked shorts and a white button-down shirt rolled up at the sleeves. "Sit down," she said, gesturing at a cushiony chair next to the desk.

Violet smiled, waiting for him to say more, resisting the urge to turn on the screen and peek at the story. She was really itching to get back to it; she was just at the part where Hayes and Rose were deciding if they wanted to go to an after-party at the beach. But Violet felt curious, too. Why was Jay here?

Jay nodded and sat down, looking a little uncomfortable. "Well," he began. "I have two tickets to a really cool lecture at USC. A neuroscience professor opened it up to the public. She's going to talk about the brain and creativity." Jay pointed to the laptop. "I thought you might be interested, since you're writing and all."

Creativity and the brain. Violet thought back to her night of polishing her fingernails, eating apples, and watching TV—anything to jump-start her brain into action. It might be helpful.

"Are you interested in writing, too?" she asked. "Or something in the arts?"

"No." Jay laughed. "I guess it's the opposite. I love science, really any kind. It's amazing how it explains the world, and it's amazing how it can change it. I'm taking some AP summer classes—chemistry and bio."

He went on to explain how that would free up time for different classes next year, more specialized ones "like neuroscience and orgo."

"Orgo?"

"Organic chemistry."

Violet had to admit she was impressed. She wasn't even sure what organic chemistry was, or neuroscience for that matter. And he seemed so excited by it all—the lecture, the classes, the learning.

"Do you want to go? It starts at eight."

"Oh, it's tonight?" Violet felt her body shift closer to the keyboard, her mind telling her to keep writing. "I'm sorry, Jay, but I should really keep working. I'm in the groove now, and I'd hate to lose the flow."

"Oh sure. Not a big deal at all. Just thought I'd ask, you know, a last-minute thing." He spoke quickly, trying to sound casual, but Violet sensed his feelings were hurt. He seemed nice, so that was the last thing she wanted to do.

"Maybe we can hang out another time?" she said.

Jay lifted his head and smiled. "That would be great." He was smiling as he left, and Violet hoped he'd understood what she'd meant . . . or what she thought she'd meant anyway: Hang out as friends.

Why were emotions so complicated? She wanted this summer to be all about work, but she felt a pull toward Hayes, and she wasn't sure why exactly. She was getting to know him, so maybe the feelings were real, but maybe she liked the idea of it, too—Violet Reeves with a celebrity all the girls were crushing on.

When it came right down to it, she was Hayes's assistant. That was all. And here was this perfectly nice, cute boy actually asking her out, and she'd turned him down. Sure, she'd said "no" because she wanted to concentrate on her writing. But it was fanfic, not a screenplay, and more to the point, Hayes Grier fanfic. To be honest, she was so into it because it made her feel closer to Hayes.

Hayes, who might be with Coco. Hayes, who may be the next big movie star. Violet groaned. She and Hayes would never be together. She had a celebrity crush, that was all, like all the other sixteen-year-old girls, and that didn't mean a thing.

Still she had fanfic Hayes. And that Hayes would never kiss Coco!

Violet opened her laptop and went back to writing.

Early the next morning, Violet was back on set, handing out TJ's notes to the cast and crew.

She hadn't seen Hayes yet. When she'd arrived at the studio, he was already in makeup, and TJ had corralled her right away. He'd said Hayes wouldn't really need her for a while; could she take care of a few things for him?

Violet had to say yes. But she'd been hoping to pull Hayes aside to go over everything from yesterday. TJ had just assumed they'd already talked. Time was ticking away, and she needed to meet with Hayes sooner rather than later.

Next, TJ had her lead a new group of extras to the cafeteria set. She was just leaving when Hayes flagged her down. "I've been looking all over for you," he said. "We still need to run those lines and go over the schedule."

"I know!" she said. "Let's go."

They walked to Hayes's trailer, not speaking, Violet

hurrying to keep up. Inside, they sat on the couch, a wide space between them. Was this the same guy who'd said, "I'd love to stay with you"? Had something changed?

"Well, you're here at the lot tomorrow," Violet told him, going through the call sheet. "You have an early call time. A car will pick you up at 5:15 a.m. on the dot." She rattled through the specifics as Hayes listened, occasionally asking a question.

Violet couldn't help but notice Hayes wasn't making eye contact. Maybe it was her imagination, but he seemed tense, almost angry.

Was he annoyed she'd been busy with other things while he was looking for her? Maybe he saw her with TJ and rethought the whole motorcycle incident, deciding she was trying to boss him around. Becoming a mini TJ.

She had to clear the air.

"Uh, Hayes?"

"Yeah?" He flipped through the schedule and barely looked up.

"You know, I feel kind of bad about yesterday, how I came down so hard on you about riding the bike. I didn't mean to be overbearing or mean. The last thing I want to do is take away your freedom." She paused. "I know how important that is to you."

Now he was staring at her, and Violet felt a warmth spread down to her toes.

"You got it—that's exactly why I like to ride. The speed, the wind, the feeling I can go anywhere and do anything— fast. But I totally understand why you didn't want me to get on the bike. It's all good. I'm just a little preoccupied now, thinking about the big final scene that's coming up soon. Anyway," he went on, "I didn't mean to give you that impression. Can I make it up to you? I'm going to invite people over tonight, just to chill and celebrate everything— you know, being in California, the movie. It won't be a big deal, a few close friends."

He leaned in closer, and Violet's stomach dropped. But he was just flicking a crumb off her shoulder. "You should definitely come. It would be nice to see each other off the lot."

"Okay." Violet hoped she sounded casual, as if she were invited to celebrity homes all the time.

"And bring anyone you like. I'll text the address."

"Hayes!" A production assistant was suddenly at the door. "You're on in five."

"Right. See you later?" Hayes asked Violet.

Not trusting her voice, she nodded. Then she hurriedly texted Mia. *Cancel any plans for tonight!* she wrote.

Immediately, she got a response.

Why?

We're invited to Hayes's house, along with a few close friends.

What about your writing? Mia texted back. *Thought you'd be staying in every night to work.*

Violet knew she was teasing her about turning down Jay's invitation.

I can take one night off, right?

Soon, Violet was done for the day. She walked outside the lot to wait for Mia to pick her up, but she couldn't keep still. She paced up and down the street, her stomach churning with nervous excitement. She had to settle down. A party was just a party—even in the Hollywood Hills. Hayes included her to be nice, to smooth over any friction.

"He's turning into a friend," Violet said out loud. "A very cute one. But really just a friend."

She remembered Hayes leaning close to her. The way he looked deep in her eyes when she talked about freedom. She shivered.

"Just a friend," she repeated firmly.

CHAPTER NINE

"MIA, HOW DO you think this would look on me?" Violet held up a sheer filmy minidress the color of pink cotton candy.

The girls were in Mia's bedroom, figuring out what to wear to Hayes's house that night.

"It would look great, but the color is all wrong for a laid-back scene. You need something more understated, like you just came back from work and threw on the first thing you saw in your closet."

"But it's your closet," Violet pointed out, grinning. "And it's hard to remember what the first thing even was—your clothes are all over the place."

An assortment of dresses, shorts, jeans, and tops littered the room. Shoes, sandals, and one lone boot were piled high on the bed.

"Okay, okay, don't take me literally." Mia giggled. She tossed Violet a pair of light blue overall shorts and dark blue tank. "Try this. It's cute and cool at the same time. Or wait. How about this?" She picked up a simple off-the-shoulder ivory-colored cotton dress, gathered at the waist. "For more of a classic-girl-next-door-who-can-be-sexy-too look."

"What about this?" Violet picked up a T-shirt dress from the floor, shifting clothes around. "Oh!" She'd uncovered her phone in the process. She glanced at the screen, then took a longer look. "Oh my God! Mia! Read this!"

Together, the girls bent over Violet's phone. *HollywoodWriter310, whoever you are, you have the most raw talent I've ever seen—in or out of Hollywood.*

"It's from someone named Lydia Jacobs," Mia said. "Why does that name sound familiar?"

"Only because she's the biggest, most powerful agent in the world," Violet crowed. "Listen!" She pulled the phone away from Mia to scroll down the screen. "She sent tons of messages. 'If you let me represent you, you'll have the career of your dreams.' 'Sign with me and you can write your own ticket.'" Violet laughed, giddy with excitement. "Get it, Mia? *Write* my own ticket?"

"Here's another one. 'Your writing draws people in, the response is out of this galaxy—get in touch ASAP.'"

Violet and Mia skipped around the room, kicking up clothes as they went. "Can you believe this?" Violet broke away to flop on the bed, pushing aside the pile of sandals. "I know I've been getting tons and tons of attention . . . people writing incredible reviews, begging—I mean really begging!—me to continue. I've been getting so many raves—"

She paused to acknowledge Mia's quiet groan. Maybe she did sound a little full of herself. But so what? Maybe she deserved to.

"But never in a million years," she continued, "did I think something like this would happen. Lydia Jacobs wants to work with me! Do you know she represents Carmen Gomes? And Robby McEntire? I don't know about writers . . . but if she has any, I'm sure they're huge, too. And I could be one of them."

"Well, yes," Mia agreed. "But then won't you have to tell Lydia who you are?"

"Of course," Violet agreed. "How else would she know who—" Violet stopped short. "Oh," she said slowly. She slumped into a chair. "Then everyone would know who wrote those stories. Maybe even . . ."

"Hayes Grier," Mia finished. "And you said it could be an issue for him."

"Well, I said maybe," Violet conceded. "But I can't let my fans down, can I? And there's always a chance he won't ever find out."

Mia sighed. "Listen, I'm your biggest fan. You know I love your writing. But you can't keep this from him any longer. It wouldn't be right. And it could definitely be trouble if he finds out on his own. You have to tell Hayes the truth before you get in touch with Lydia."

"I don't know . . ." Violet twisted a long curl around her finger.

"Please, Violet," Mia begged. "You owe him that much."

"You're right, my little conscience," Violet told her, patting her head. "I'll tell him tonight—everything from my writer's block and why I started writing, to my messages from Lydia Jacobs."

Violet shook her head, wishing she could just sweep everything under the rug and have fun tonight. It took a lot for her to talk to Hayes and clear the air this afternoon. And the fanfic was so much bigger. It could change the way he thought about her.

No matter what he thought about her now—and she didn't have a clue—what would he think after finding out she was using him to write fan fiction?

"Here." Mia handed Violet the overalls. "This will give an open and honest vibe." She grabbed a T-shirt for herself. It was an original Mia design, a soft patchwork of fabric squares with sayings like, "Each new sunrise promises a new beginning," "Stand Strong," "It's okay to be afraid, but try anyway." Quickly, the cousins dressed and headed out the door.

Excitement gripped Violet like a vise. They were going to Hayes Grier's Hollywood party. And on top of that, she had to have a serious discussion with him, come clean about the stories.

After tonight, she thought, *nothing may ever be the same.*

Violet and Mia drove through the winding streets of Hollywood Hills. Carved from canyon sides, the road twisted in an upward spiral. At the top, Violet knew, stood the iconic Hollywood Sign.

She gazed out the window as they passed houses built on stilts and mansions half-hidden by trees. Narrow streets brought them higher and higher until Mia slowed the car and peered down a long, straight driveway. They couldn't see the house.

"This is it," she declared.

"Are you sure?" Violet asked. Cars lined the driveway on either side. There was one spot left, at the very end.

"Yup." Mia pulled neatly into the empty space. "Looks like we're the last to arrive."

"Hopefully," Violet said. She couldn't imagine how many people must already be inside. Her preparty excitement quickly faded, leaving a hollow feeling in her stomach. With all these cars, she highly doubted it was an intimate gathering of close friends. More like a packed, blow-out party.

Mia eyed her. "So are we still on for this?"

Violet nodded. They were already there, after all.

The girls got out of the car and began to walk. At the end, the driveway curved, revealing a sprawling one-level home, every room brightly lit. Music blared, a fast-paced rap song Violet didn't recognize, and the sound of laughter echoed through the trees.

Mia grabbed her hand, squeezing it twice. Taking a deep breath, they stepped through the open double doors.

The entrance led straight to a huge sunken living room. A DJ sat at a booth, tapping at a laptop. People lounged on white leather couches. Some couples were dancing. Violet peered around. The party seemed to push into halls leading deeper into the house.

Violet and Mia sidled tentatively inside. The living room's floor-to-ceiling windows opened onto a patio and backyard. People were jumping into a kidney-shaped pool, complete with a slide and high diving board. Violet saw a taco truck parked on the grass, a line of people waiting.

"This is too much," Mia whispered. She could have

shouted, and no one would have heard. The noise level rose even higher as a bikini-clad girl did a perfect swan dive into the deep end.

Speechless, Violet could only nod. There were so many people, most of them girls, and all of them Hollywood beautiful. It didn't seem real. It was like a scene straight out of a movie. Maybe one of those old '80s movies, where the ultrarich guy threw a party and embarrassed the hero, who came from a poor but loving family and didn't belong with the faster, hipper crowd. She'd definitely be playing that fish-out-of-water role.

Would the movie heroine feel the way she was feeling right now? She didn't want to come right out and define it, even to herself. But it was a feeling in the pit of her stomach when she gazed at these tanned, together girls. After a few minutes, she found the strength to label it. Jealousy. Were all these girls Hayes's close, intimate friends?

"Violet!" Hayes was moving through the crowd. "You made it!"

At the sight of Hayes, Violet's confusion melted away. He was barefoot, wearing black shorts that Violet thought could be swim trunks and a blinding white shirt, unbuttoned. "I'm so happy you're here!" He looked at Mia, and Violet quickly introduced them.

"Hey," he said. "Violet's talked about you a lot. It's great to meet you." He walked around her slowly, reading all the fabric patches. "This is one amazing tee," he said. "Who's the designer?"

"Mia designed it herself!" Violet put in quickly. "Isn't it great?"

"It is!"

"Thanks," Mia said quietly, beaming.

"Hey, Tez!" Hayes shouted into the crowd. "You've got to see this!"

As if on command, Tez materialized out of nowhere. "What's up?"

"This is Violet's cousin, Mia. What do you think of her T-shirt?"

Tez eyed the shirt up and down, giving a long, low whistle, and Mia blushed.

"Walk around," Hayes said. "There's more on the back."

Tez loped around Mia, then stood in front of her, arms crossed over his chest. "Definitely dope."

"This is what I've been talking about," Hayes said excitedly. "I want to totally revamp my merchandise line, and this could be big! It's spot-on innovative and different."

"It could definitely work with your stuff," Tez agreed. "We should get together," he told Mia. He paused, grinning as Mia blushed again. "And talk about creating new designs for my man."

Mia gave a little yelp, and now Violet was smiling wider

than Tez. That was amazing news; it could be a real break for Mia.

"You must have an eye for what's hot," Tez was saying to Mia, edging closer.

And maybe, Violet thought, *there's more here than a business interest*. An image flashed, unbidden, through her mind: Tez and Mia double-dating with her and Hayes, the four of them stretched out on one blanket at the Santa Monica beach.

"Want to grab a bite at the taco truck?" Tez asked Mia. She nodded, grinning, as he reached for her hand to guide her through the living room.

Quickly, Violet put the fantasy out of her mind. For all she knew, Tez and Mia were more of a sure thing than she and Hayes.

But now—if she ignored all the other girls hanging around—Violet and Hayes were alone. "What should we do?" he asked.

Violet's heart beat faster. He wasn't looking at any of those girls. He was looking at *her*!

Hayes swept his arm toward the opposite corner of the room. "There's a photo booth over there. Should we strike a pose?" He raised his eyebrows and smiled.

A photo booth! With everything else going on, Violet hadn't even noticed the curtained-off space. "Sure!"

Moments later, Hayes held the curtain open, and they

squeezed into the small, cozy booth. When Hayes pulled the curtain closed, darkness fell, and a charged silence fell between them. Violet felt like they were the only two people in the world.

"Should we do silly, serious, or crazy?" She felt like she had to whisper.

Hayes leaned closer to whisper back, "Let's start with goofy." His breath felt hot against her ear.

Violet giggled as he drew back to make a face, crossing his eyes and baring his teeth. She twisted her mouth into a one-sided smirk and wrinkled her nose. Flash—one photo done. They went on to genuine smiles, Hayes tickling Violet so she was laughing hysterically, and then one when they weren't even posing—just looking deeply into each other's eyes.

"Caught on film!" Hayes joked when they looked over the photos, still sitting close together. A few people opened the curtain and peered at them curiously. Violet didn't care what they thought. She was having too much fun.

"You take one." Hayes handed Violet a strip. "And I'll keep the other. I'm going to save it."

He was going to save their photos? Violet's heart hammered in her chest. That had to mean something. "Me, too," Violet said, sure she was blushing.

"You know, pictures are really important to me," Hayes went on as they stepped out of the booth. People were calling out to him, a few girls actually tugged on his arm, but Hayes ignored them, standing still, close to Violet.

"I'm away from my family so much. And I'm so busy, it's hard to connect with everyone back home. But pictures . . . they're like a little piece of my family that I can always have with me."

Violet thought about her mom and dad, clear across the country, and how sometimes before she went to sleep, she scrolled through albums on her phone just to see their faces. She couldn't believe Hayes felt the same way.

"Hayes, bro, move away and let someone else get into the booth." Tez was standing right in front of them, Mia by his side. Violet had been so wrapped up in her thoughts—and in Hayes—she hadn't seen them approach.

"No, you guys take your time," Mia said, pulling Tez back to give them space. "He's just annoyed the taco truck ran out of guacamole."

"We were done anyway." Hayes gave a kind of salute and held out his hand for Violet. "Want to go somewhere we can get away from these jerks? Oh," he added quickly. "I didn't mean you, Mia."

"That's okay," Mia laughed. "I have the feeling Tez is jerk enough for both of us."

Still holding Violet's hand, Hayes led her outside. "How about going up to the Hollywood Sign?" he asked. "I have a tip from a buddy that they're filming there tonight. So for the first time in years, the sign will be lit." He grinned. "He gave me a supersecret route and told me where to park. If we're lucky, we'll be able to see some stars through all the smog."

Stars! Smog! He remembered their conversation. Violet caught her breath. Of course, she realized, she could remember each one of their conversations—even the ones where he asked her to pick up a smoothie. But still, it was thrilling. More and more, she was allowing herself to have feelings for him.

Tonight, she couldn't deny the attraction. But before she could even think about that . . . about what could happen at the Hollywood Sign . . . she had to tell him about the fanfic. She only hoped he would understand.

CHAPTER TEN

VIOLET WAS QUIET driving up the mountain, letting Hayes carry the conversation. He talked about *The Midnight Hawk* for a bit. Then he switched to Tez, saying how he's hard to keep up with, but it seemed Mia wouldn't have a problem. "And she's mad talented," Hayes went on. "She's really cool."

Hayes liked her BFF. He thought she was cool. He totally got why Mia was so great. Violet smiled, feeling her heart expand.

Hayes swung the car into a dead-end street, then turned off the engine. A bright white light filtered through the trees.

The Hollywood Sign, Violet guessed. They walked a bit, and the light grew brighter and brighter until there it was before them, letters blazing, the darkness surrounding them like a cozy blanket.

"Let's sit here," Hayes said, leading Violet to a low stone wall.

From here, the letters seemed to stretch right up to the sky. They could see each one, a full view of HOLLYWOOD just a bit above them, yet they were far enough away to feel alone. The film crew must be working furiously at the sign's base, Violet thought. But she couldn't see or hear a thing.

Violet twisted to look down the mountainside. LA spread before them like a tapestry, its own lights twinkling brightly.

The world seemed to shine just for her and Hayes. Violet turned to Hayes, readying herself to tell him about the fan fiction.

Instead, she found herself looking deep into his eyes. "It's all so beautiful," she said softly.

Hayes nodded. "Now look all the way up," he instructed. "Let's see if we can spot constellations."

Violet peered at the sky, but only a few stars showed through the smog and clouds.

"On second thought," Hayes joked, "keep looking down. The city lights might be the best we can do."

"Let's not give up," Violet said. Suddenly, she grabbed his arm. "Look!" A shooting star arced over their heads, a streak of glowing light that came and went so quickly, Violet wasn't sure it had been real. "Did you see it?" she asked. "Was it really there?"

"I did see it," Hayes murmured. "And I made a wish." He turned his body, leaning into Violet, his lips parted for a kiss.

Violet moved toward him, her heart pounding, a sweet sensation sweeping through her body like her own personal shooting star. But she couldn't kiss him. Not yet! They hadn't talked yet. It just wouldn't be right.

"I . . . I can't," she said, forcing herself to pull back. "I have to tell you—"

"No worries," Hayes said quickly. "You don't have to explain. I get it. I just misread things, that's all. Saw some signals that weren't really there." He shrugged.

Violet's mind was racing. What should she do? He seemed disappointed, but he was acting so nice about it, Violet's heart ached.

"No!" Violet said. She had to explain. She had to start right from the beginning. "You know I've been trying to write, and—"

Hayes's cell phone rang. He pressed IGNORE and turned to her, his eyebrows raised in a question. But his phone rang again. This time, he silenced it, but the phone kept vibrating. He glanced at the screen. "It's Tez," he said. "It may be important."

"Answer it. Really."

Hayes swiped at the screen and held the phone to his ear. Before he could even say hello, Violet heard Tez shouting. "Bro, you've got to get back here. Things are getting crazy. One dude broke that photo in your bedroom—you know, the one with your whole family sitting in your dining room for Thanksgiving."

"No!" Hayes spoke loudly, too. "Is it just the glass? Is the photo okay?"

"I'm not sure. Somehow it smashed to the ground, and the guy went and stomped on it, too. The frame snapped in half. I think the picture is torn."

"Do me a favor and put it in a safe place," Hayes told Tez. "I'll be right back.

"My mom gave me that picture and frame, right before I came here," Hayes explained to Violet, hanging up. "She wrote this whole inscription on the back. We need to go to the house; I want to see if I can fix it."

"Of course." Violet jumped to her feet.

"But you were about to say something." Hayes paused.

Clearly, Hayes was upset; Violet knew pictures were so important to him. If she told him about the fanfic now, it would just make him feel worse. She couldn't make this night any harder for him.

"No, it's okay. It can wait. Really. Come on!" Violet said, pulling him back to the car.

She would hold off telling him. Waiting wouldn't change anything. The fanfic wasn't going anywhere, and hopefully neither was Hayes. She'd find the perfect time, then tell him everything. They'd pick up where they left off, and this time she wouldn't pull back from the kiss. And maybe that kiss would tell her what she needed to know, too: that her feelings were real—for the real Hayes Grier. That he wasn't just a celebrity crush.

Then everything would be great between them. It would be fine.

At least that's what she told herself.

"You didn't say a word the whole way home!" Mia was sitting at the kitchen table, digging into a big bowl of raspberry tea organic ice cream. She pushed an extra spoon at Violet sitting across the table, but Violet pushed it back dejectedly. "Does that mean Hayes got mad when he heard about the fanfic?" Mia pressed.

"I didn't get a chance to tell him," Violet mumbled.

"What?" Mia jerked to attention, overturning the bowl. Pink soupy ice cream spread across the marble table.

"Here." Violet reached for a paper towel and mopped it up, catching it just before it dripped on the floor.

"Don't try and distract me by cleaning!" Mia snapped. "Did you really not talk about it?"

"I couldn't," Violet said miserably. "I was about to—I swear, Mia!—but then he tried to kiss me."

"And?" Mia drew out the word, meaning she wanted to hear everything . . . about the kiss . . . about the discussion. The problem was, there was nothing to tell. There wasn't a kiss, and there wasn't any discussion. And Violet couldn't decide which was more upsetting.

Quickly, Violet explained how she'd wanted to talk to Hayes before anything happened between them. But just when she was about to begin, he went in for the kiss, and she stopped it. Then she tried a second time, but Tez kept calling. And when Hayes finally answered, Tez told him about the photo.

"I knew it wasn't the right time," Violet finished. She slumped in her chair. "There. Now I've told you everything that happened. What do you think?"

"I think you really need some ice cream." Mia got up to get another bowl and dished out scoops. "I understand," she told Violet. "I get why you didn't talk to him. I do. But there's never going to be a right time. The sooner you do it, the better. Do it at work tomorrow. Just get through it. Pretend it's a homework assignment, maybe."

Violet rolled her eyes. "That's so lame, Mia. But I know, I know. I just have to do it. Do you think I totally messed up tonight? Did Hayes think I was rejecting him?" Violet paused. "That's what I really want to know."

"Well, there's only one way to find out. Clear the air. Be honest. Talk about the fanfic. Then ask him!"

The next morning, Violet arrived at work earlier than usual. She'd barely slept the night before, thinking and worrying. Finally, she'd decided to just get up and had gotten out of bed at 5:30 to shower and dress.

The quicker she told Hayes about the fanfic, the quicker it would all be over. She felt ready, almost eager to get it off her chest. Maybe after, they could go back to being whatever they almost were last night. Friends? More than friends?

But even at that early hour, it seemed everyone had beat her to the lot. The place was in complete chaos. Loud voices rang out amid the uproar. People rushed here and there in a frenzy. Dozens of panicked production assistants talked excitedly on their phones.

TJ, meanwhile, was inhaling and exhaling into a paper bag—using it like a makeshift inhaler—in between shouting out commands. Violet could barely hear herself think.

Finally, Violet cornered Derek, another intern. "What's going on?"

Derek paused long enough to say, "We're supposed to be filming part of that big motorcycle scene today. You know the rest will be done on location?"

"Yes, I know, I know." Violet waved at the back lot; a

long line of cars stood behind a truck, its long trailer opened at the back. "Hawk" would ride his motorcycle out of the truck, jump over the cars, and land in a small empty space between a mobile home and an SUV. Then he'd spin quickly around. Wind machines had been set up to give the impression of movement. But even with stationary cars, it was a tricky stunt.

"I do work here, you know," Violet told Derek. She couldn't help but be a little snippy. Lack of sleep will do that to you.

"Well, the stunt guy should have been here an hour ago. We're trying to track him down or find a replacement."

That was bad news. Any delay would cost a lot of money. But it seemed half the crew was already working on that. And Violet knew what—or whom—she should focus on. Hayes. She had to make sure he was all right. That was her job.

She searched the lot, then tried his trailer, then hurried back to the freeway scene. Finally, she spied him, trying to calm TJ down and offering suggestions about the stunt—none of which seemed to be well received.

"Really, TJ," Hayes was saying. He sounded nervous, unsure of himself, but determined to speak his mind. "I think you should get a couple more trucks, and park them in front of that one. When the stunt guy gets here, he'll tell you the same thing. It's much safer for him to ride on top of the trucks and take off over the cars than just come out of that truck and jump them. Or maybe make the trailer longer. Yeah, extend the trailer, or open it up on the other end so the guy can ride into the truck, then go. That could do it, too."

TJ took another breath into the bag. "Listen, Hayes, I know you're trying to help. But right now we have to find a stuntman. Period."

Hayes held up his hands. "Okay, I get it. I'm here if you need me, though." He walked toward the craft service table, and Violet followed.

"Hayes!" she said. "How are you doing? Are you okay? I mean, with the shoot," she added hurriedly. She didn't want him to think she was talking about the nonkiss last night—not when there was so much going on right now.

"I just wish this whole thing was straightened out," Hayes told her, "so we can start shooting. If we wait too much longer, we'll lose an entire day."

"Maybe you don't have to wait," Violet said slowly, an idea hitting her with such force, she actually shouted. "You can do the stunt."

"Me?" Hayes looked at her like she was speaking a foreign language. "You know that can't happen, V."

When she heard the nickname, Violet's heart leaped. Maybe things were going to be fine between them.

"TJ said I couldn't do any motorcycle stunts. And you," he said, grinning, "are supposed to make sure of it."

Violet shook her head. "Not anymore, I'm not. I've seen you riding the bike. You have amazing control. And if TJ takes your suggestion, it will be that much safer, right?"

"Right," Hayes said uncertainly.

"Besides," Violet went on. She gazed deep into his eyes and held his hand tightly. "I believe in you. I know you can do this."

"You do? I can?" he said, sounding surprised.

"Yes, come on!"

"Okay!" Hayes agreed, in a stronger voice, standing straighter. "I think I can, too!"

Violet gripped him even harder and pulled him over to TJ, who was standing a few feet away, popping TUMS into his mouth.

"TJ, we need to talk to you," Violet said. She stood next to Hayes so they blocked any escape. "We know what to do about the stunt."

"You do?" TJ gave a half-snort. "Then you'd be the only ones in the entire studio."

"Hayes can do it."

TJ rubbed his eyes tiredly. "You know I want to keep him safe."

"I do know that. But if you listen to his suggestion—adding trucks or doing something about the trailer for more momentum—he will be safe."

TJ shook his head. "It's still too dangerous."

Violet nudged Hayes, and he stepped forward. "TJ, I know I can do it. And you don't want to waste an entire day. Think of the schedule. Think of the money."

"It's true," TJ mused. "It would be way too expensive to move this scene to another day. This setup cost so much already."

He waved two assistant directors over, and they discussed how to rework the scene. Violet overheard the phrases "unhook the trailer," "open the front," "add a ramp," and "build up speed."

TJ turned to Hayes. "I hate to do this, but I'm saying yes." He eyed Hayes. "Just get a helmet—and fast, before I change my mind."

One hour later, everything was set. The trailer had been rebuilt and a long ramp added to the open front, hidden from the cameras.

Hayes stood next to Violet, the helmet under his arm, tapping his toe against the floor with a frenzied beat. His nervous energy was almost tangible—so strong, Violet felt she could reach out and touch it.

"You holding up okay?" she asked.

"Sure, just another day on the job," he joked. "It's not as if this is the first time I'm doing this stunt." He hit his head with his palm. "Oh wait, it is!" He tried to smile at Violet. "I am nervous," he admitted softly, "and I didn't think I would be. You know I always wanted to do this! But now so much is riding on it—"

"No pun intended." Violet wanted to make Hayes smile for real, and he did, visibly relaxing as he laughed.

"I'm afraid I'll mess up," Hayes continued. He waved at the set, taking in the cast and crew. "I don't want to disappoint everyone."

"You won't mess up. You did the hardest part already, convincing TJ. Now just do what you normally do—ride like the wind. There's not a doubt in my mind you'll be great." She held up her hand to his chin, tilting his head so he looked her in the eyes and couldn't see anything else but her belief in him.

"Everyone on set," TJ called. "We're starting in . . ." He glanced at his watch. "Now!"

"So go out there and ride," Violet told Hayes, holding his gaze.

Hayes took a deep breath, grinned, and fastened the helmet. He strode toward the bike, then turned back. Quickly, he drew Violet in for a hug. "Thanks, V."

Minutes later, everyone had found their mark. Lights and cameras turned on. Crew members crowded around the scene. Hayes sat on the bike at the far end of the lot.

"Take one!" called the assistant director, snapping the board.

"Action!" TJ cried.

Violet couldn't see much. But she heard an engine gun and the sound of rushing wind. Then Hayes came roaring through the trailer . . . flying into the air, rising over one car . . . two cars . . . three . . .

Violet held her breath as he cleared the final SUV, then spun around neatly.

"Cut!" called TJ. "That's a wrap!"

The set erupted in cheers. ADs high-fived PAs. The craft guys whistled.

"You nailed it, Hayes!" TJ cried.

For one long moment, Hayes just sat on the bike, not moving. Finally, he switched off the engine and put down the kickstand. People were rushing over to congratulate him, but he skirted them to find Violet. He folded her into a long, close hug.

Violet breathed in his scent, a heady mix of exhaust, leather, and orange peels.

"Enough of that!" TJ said, coming over, playfully pulling them apart. "We have to make up for lost time. Everyone, enough celebrating!" he called out. "Get ready for the next scene—Hawk's dad confronting Devon in a coffee shop."

The set quieted as people went their separate ways. "As for you," TJ told Hayes, "I'm impressed. You really did a great job. You have the afternoon off. So relax."

"Thanks, TJ," Hayes said happily.

"Don't thank me quite yet," TJ shot back. "You have that big emotional scene at the end of the movie coming up soon. And that, my friend, will be your true test."

TJ sauntered off, dropping the empty TUMS container in the trash.

Hayes and Violet exchanged looks. Violet knew that final scene was weighing heavily on Hayes. She wished TJ hadn't brought it up now, not when he was feeling so confident.

As if reading her mind, Hayes said, "Don't worry, V. I'm not going to let TJ get to me. I mean, did you see that jump? I feel like I can do anything." He paused. "At least on a motorcycle."

"Yeah, bro!" Tez was suddenly standing in front of them.

How does he do that? Violet wondered. *He's always appearing out of and disappearing into thin air.*

"You did an amazing job out there!" Tez smiled and nodded at Violet like they were old friends and said, "Hey you." Violet smiled back, happy to be included in the inner circle.

Tez dodged around Hayes like he was dribbling a basketball. He feigned taking a shot. "Next time we play hoops? I want you on my team for a change!"

"I'll think about it," Hayes told him, grinning. "But no promises."

"Seems like you're on a roll." Tez settled down and lounged against a wall. "People are talking 'bout you, dude.

Have you seen this crazy fanfic everyone is obsessing over?"

"You mean those made-up stories about me?" Hayes shook his head in disbelief. "I just found out about them this morning before all this crazy on-set stuff happened. I'd just posted this new pic of Zan and me on Instagram." Hayes flicked on his phone to show Violet and Tez the picture. The two were posed in front of Hayes's trailer, both wearing motorcycle helmets and leather jackets. "And my followers were going crazy for those stories in the comments section."

Violet gulped. "H-h-have you read any of it yet?"

"Nah, I haven't had time, you should know that." He elbowed her, grinning happily. "But I'm cool with it."

"You are?" Violet felt like a load had been lifted from her shoulders.

"Sure, so long as the stuff I want to keep private stays private."

Violet caught her breath. What did that mean exactly? She wished she had an answer—a road map to Hayes's heart, pointing out which areas were off-limits and which were open to the public.

"Okay, catch you later," Tez said, reaching out to Hayes for a one-armed bro hug. He smiled at Violet. "Me and your girl have a meeting, to get started on some merch ideas."

"Hey, that's great!" Violet said absently, waving as he strolled away.

"What have you got going on?" Hayes asked Violet.

"Me?" Violet squeaked, thinking maybe somehow he knew she was the fanfic writer and planned to post more stories. But that was ridiculous. He had no way of knowing. And she had plenty of time to tell him. He'd admitted he was too busy to read them. It was possible he'd even like them. Of course, it was just as possible he wouldn't . . .

"Yes, you," Hayes prompted.

"Whatever you need done is what I've got going on. I'm your assistant, remember?"

Hayes smacked his head. "That's right, I forgot. But do you think you can get off the lot and come shopping with me? I have a huge red-carpet event tonight—the premiere of *Hearts and Darts*—and I haven't a clue what I should wear."

Hearts and Darts was a small independent movie that was getting a lot of press—two American twenty-somethings meet in a London pub, playing darts. Violet thought it looked really good. But she wasn't thinking about the movie now. She was thinking about Hayes's invitation.

"You want my help choosing an outfit?" Violet said, surprised.

"Sure. You've got great style."

Violet looked down at her jean shorts and bright red sneakers, the same color as her formfitting T-shirt. She'd been so bleary-eyed that morning, she'd just picked clothes off the floor. Luckily they matched. She looked fine but certainly not hip or fashionable.

Hayes must still like her—at least as a friend—if he was letting himself believe she had style. He probably just wanted company and hoped Mia's taste had rubbed off on her.

"You're on!"

CHAPTER ELEVEN

VIOLET HAD DRIVEN through Beverly Hills before; she'd seen the most upscale neighborhood in LA many times. More specifically, she'd been down Rodeo Drive, a wide boulevard lined with palm trees and luxury shops and restaurants. With her uncle or Mia at the wheel, she'd gaped at passing store windows and the beautiful people strolling by.

But she'd never actually *walked* down the streets. Now, even with tourists strolling along, taking pictures, she felt a little out of her element. She overheard a husband and wife pronounce the street name like the regular rodeo, as in cowboys riding the range.

At least she knew it was pronounced Roh-DAY-oh Drive, Violet thought. That was one good thing. And after a few minutes of casual window-shopping, she relaxed. When a group of young girls rushed over, asking for Hayes's autograph, she stepped back. Then she smiled at an older couple who were looking at her questioningly. *I'm nobody important*, she wanted to tell them. *But I'm with somebody who is.*

"I think it's time to go undercover," Hayes told Violet when the girls moved on. They rushed back to the car for baseball caps and sunglasses, Hayes insisting Violet wear them, too.

Then they ducked into a narrow cobblestone alley with small shops on either side. To Violet, the street looked like a movie set, and suddenly she felt like she was costarring in a film, cameras capturing her every move.

If this were a movie, Violet thought, their Rodeo Drive scene would be a montage of moments . . .

Hayes leading her into store after store . . . Violet skimming through a rack . . . explaining to a salesperson they were looking for a red-carpet outfit . . .

Hayes and Violet laughing over striped slacks that looked more like a prison uniform than a fashion statement . . .

Hayes preening in front of a mirror, modeling a flowing silk shirt and fedora . . . showing off a long leather jacket that he said made him feel like a couch . . . trying on a white-on-white tuxedo . . . then finally settling on a more casual tuxedo—more of a blazer with green lapels, a matching green V-necked T-shirt, tailored black slacks, and white sneakers.

The montage would show them laughing . . . their eyes meeting in the mirror . . . their fingers brushing when they reached for the same shirt.

Violet felt almost giddy. She was having so much fun; Hayes was acting perfectly normal, and there'd been no awkwardness about the night before. It probably helped, she realized, that they'd worked together to fix the *Midnight Hawk* scene, and that it turned out so well.

But was it all so relaxed because they were firmly in the "friend zone"? She thought back to the moments when they touched, when their eyes met. Her stomach tightened just remembering.

"Come on, V. Let's get out of here."

They left the last shop side by side, Hayes swinging his shopping bag back and forth. "That outfit is dope," he told Violet. "Tonight I'll be the best-dressed guy on the red carpet." He turned to Violet. "Did you say something?"

"No." Violet blushed. "That was my stomach." She'd barely eaten all day, just a few crackers with cheese from the craft table that morning. "Ugh," she added. "Excuse me."

"That was you?" Hayes laughed. "I thought it was me. Listen, we're both hungry. Shopping is like exercise. It should be an Olympic sport. How about we get something to eat? I can take you to my favorite place."

Once again, Violet looked down at her shorts and sneakers. She wasn't exactly dressed for a ritzy Rodeo Drive restaurant, but she was feeling a little reckless. And how could she turn down the chance to spend more time with Hayes?

"Lead the way!"

"Heavenly Cupcakes." Violet stood outside the small shop, Hayes by her side, and laughed. The sign featured a pink-frosted cupcake topped by a golden halo. "I love it!"

Aha! she told herself. *I got it right this time. I didn't say "I love you." I said "I love it!"*

And she did love it. She was thrilled that Hayes's favorite place wasn't a fancy restaurant where people went to see and be seen but a tiny out-of-the-way shop with just a few tables—that only served cupcakes!

"I do have a thing for cupcakes," she confided to Hayes as they settled into seats at a corner table. "In fact, I consider myself a cupcake connoisseur. I've had everything from plain vanilla with vanilla icing to salt and pepper and key lime butternut. I've even made up a list."

Hayes's eyes lit up as he handed her a menu. "An expert, eh? I'm impressed. Well, I've got to warn you, they have some pretty wild ones here, too. What looks good to you, oh knowledgeable one?"

Violet read through the items, laughing happily. "They have like a hundred different cupcakes! My uncle would love some of these—mango and vegetarian chili! Cucumber and cream cheese! And look, here's an instant classic: the PB&J cupcake! But maybe that's too mainstream. The weirder, the better, I say!"

"I'm with you, V. How about honey and ham? Or mashed potato and gravy?"

"Well, I'm thinking more sweet than savory today," Violet declared, not wanting to explain that today had been so sweet, she had to go with a light, fluffy dessert. "I'll get the raspberry marshmallow."

"Let's make that two. And it's my treat." Hayes stood up, walked close behind her, then bent to whisper in her ear, "Be right back."

Violet's ear, so close to his lips, flushed red. She couldn't turn around, sure her cheeks were bright red, too.

She heard Hayes joke with the woman behind the counter, and seconds later he was back, holding a tray with two pink-and-white-swirled cupcakes, colorful miniature marshmallows arranged on top.

Hayes placed the tray on the table, then sat back down, grinning. Violet smiled back and reached for the nearest cupcake. She unwrapped the bottom, ready to eat.

"Wait!" Hayes practically shouted. "That's no way to eat a cupcake! You can't just bite into it!"

Violet giggled. "Come on, Hayes. How else would you do it?"

"Allow me to demonstrate."

Violet sat forward, eagerly watching as Hayes took off his cupcake wrapper, then cut the cupcake in half, dividing the top from the bottom.

"Go ahead," he said. "Now you do it."

Violet picked up the knife and sliced.

"Now," Hayes went on, "carefully place the side with the icing on the bottom half, like so." He switched the two halves. "So the icing is in the middle."

Violet did the same, trying to control her giggles. "It's a cupcake sandwich!" she declared. "Now can I eat?"

"Be my guest," Hayes said grandly.

Violet bit into the creamy sweet dessert and nodded vigorously. "You're right!" she exclaimed. "It's delicious!"

Somehow the cupcake tasted better that way. Was it the crazy Hayes sandwich style that did it? Or was it just being with Hayes? Either way, it was definitely the best cupcake she'd ever had.

Back at the studio, Violet and Hayes walked past the back lot. The jimmied-up tractor-trailer truck had been removed, but other than that it looked the same—minus the hundreds of people and the crazed feeling of panic.

"I can't believe that was only this morning," Violet told Hayes. "It seems like a lifetime ago."

"I know," Hayes agreed. "I was feeling pretty anxious. But now, thanks to you, it's all good. Except . . ."

"Yes?" she prodded.

"Well, come here."

Hayes led her to another huge lot, seemingly at the top of a big hill. They climbed up and sat side by side against a log, looking out over a parking lot. "This is it," he said. "The backdrop for my big emotional moment. The final scene."

He reached for her hand. "This morning's nerves are nothing compared to how I feel about this. I'm dreading it, V. I'd rather film that motorcycle scene a million more times than try to cry on camera."

"That's really tough. Crying comes from such a personal place. It must be hard just to turn it on, on cue, and feel as if everyone can see right through you—to the well of emotion you're trying to draw from."

"That's exactly right! So many times I've seen actors bawling, and it looks so phony, like they just sniffed raw onions and turned on the tears for the camera. But other times, I've seen acting so real, and the actors so distraught, I have trouble watching, like I'm seeing something I shouldn't and learning too much about the real person." He sighed. "It's like a lose-lose proposition."

Hayes was really confiding in her. Violet wanted to tread carefully. "I don't know if it's so black-and-white," she said. "You're seeing the actors a certain way because you're an actor. When I watch a movie and see a character cry, sometimes it is almost laughably funny. But when the emotion is real, I don't think about the actor. I'm too caught up in the movie."

Hayes's eyes flashed at her words, and he stared at her so intently, Violet felt a jolt of electricity. She jumped a little, and Hayes released her hand. Now she felt an emptiness, like she'd lost something precious.

"Is that just you, though, V? Because you feel things so strongly?"

Violet shook her head. "I think people want to lose themselves in movies."

Hayes rubbed his neck, trying to work out a crick. "But what if I can't manage that? What if I'm more of a slice-some-onions-so-my-eyes-water kind of actor? It would be so transparent. It would ruin the scene—and probably the entire movie."

"Oh, Hayes." Violet couldn't help herself; she kneeled behind him, putting her hands on his shoulders and kneading them gently. It was all she could do not to wrap both arms around his chest and hold him tight. "I get that you're nervous. It's your first really big emotional scene. But you've got it in you."

Hayes twisted to look her in the eyes, and Violet's hands trembled. "I'm so comfortable around you, V. I trust you." He leaned back so their bodies were touching. "I can talk about things with you. I can open up. If you work with me, I know I could be raw. Vulnerable. I know I could do it with your help."

It was almost a declaration of some sort, and Violet felt her knees weaken. She swayed, feeling dizzy. She sat back down heavily and took a deep breath. "Of course I'll help you, Hayes."

Violet stared straight ahead, afraid to look him in the eyes again. Afraid the feelings would be too strong. "Any way I can."

Hayes bumped her with his shoulder. "Thank you, thank you." He turned toward her so she couldn't avoid eye contact. "I already know we work great together. Come to the premiere with me tonight!" he said suddenly. "You can see what I look like in my new clothes, and we'll have an amazing time."

Hayes was asking her to walk the red carpet with him! Was it a date? Or two friends going out?

Would she get photographed, too? Be featured in the newspaper as his date, while everyone wondered who this mysterious, never-before-seen girl was? *Is she an actress?* they'd ask themselves. *An old friend?*

A serious girlfriend?

Violet shook her head to clear away the thoughts. She really wasn't sure how a red-carpet event worked, and probably nobody would give her a second glance. And truth be told, she didn't really care. She just wanted to be with Hayes, to share some special moments. And she really did want to see that movie!

"I'd love to go!" she said, jumping to her feet as if they were leaving right then and there.

"Whoa, slow down," Hayes laughed. "I'll pick you up at six." He checked his watch. "Oh no! I've got to meet with TJ right now." He touched her cheek gently, and once again Violet felt faint. "But I'll see you tonight."

"O-k-kay," she said as he walked off slowly. He turned to look back at her, and Violet gave a shaky wave.

What now? Violet thought. She gazed at her hand, still trembling. Today she'd gotten to know Hayes in a whole different way. She didn't think of him as Hayes Grier, celebrity, anymore. He was Hayes Grier . . . Well, that part was a question mark. Hayes Grier, friend? Hayes Grier, potential boyfriend?

Back at the Hollywood Sign, he'd wanted to kiss her. That was clear. But maybe that was just in the moment. And when it didn't happen? The moment passed, never to come again. But now he'd asked her to the premiere. What should she think?

"Get a grip, Violet!" she said out loud. "Stop overanalyzing everything. You have a ton to do before the premiere."

She should get a new outfit; go shopping. Not on Rodeo Drive, of course, but somewhere trendy and hip, yet still reasonable. Then she'd shower and put on makeup. And, of course, tell Mia everything that had happened.

Mia was going to die. She'd want every detail, from the second Violet said hello to Hayes to—

Violet stopped. The first thing Mia would want to know about was how the fanfic talk had gone, a conversation Violet and Hayes had never had. She'd never told him about the stories! First there was the craziness on set, the realization that Hayes already knew about the site. She'd needed time to come to terms with that. But after, she'd been so excited about shopping and hanging out, about eating those crazy cupcakes, she hadn't given it another thought.

Until now.

CHAPTER TWELVE

VIOLET STOPPED AT A LITTLE, out-of-the-way Venice boutique on the way back and found a simple knee-length dress, not too tight, not too loose. It was a solid blue that matched Hayes's eyes, with a price that matched her pocketbook. The only slightly daring feature was the low, scooped-out back.

At home, she called out for Mia as soon as she walked inside.

"Hi there, my favorite niece," said Uncle Forrest, meeting her in the front hall.

"I'm your only niece," she retorted.

"True, true. But if I had a hundred, you'd still be number one."

Violet gave him a quick hug and asked, "Where's Mia?"

"She went to an art show at the last minute," Uncle Forrest said. "She won't be back until around eight." He looked at her curiously. "Anything I can help you with?"

"No, no," Violet said quickly. "I'm going out, too. To a red-carpet event and a premiere," she couldn't help but add.

"Sounds nice," said Uncle Forrest placidly, not asking any more questions.

Now, if I were going to a meditation workshop, he'd be all ears, Violet thought. But it was just as well. Talking about tonight would only make her more anxious. And it was probably better that Mia wasn't around, either. Violet would have to explain why she hadn't confessed to Hayes. But she'd talk to him tonight. Definitely. And by the time she saw Mia, everything would be straightened out. Of course, this could change things between them. Whatever might have been between them may never happen. Violet sighed as she walked up the stairs, crossing her fingers for luck.

In her room, she sat at the desk and swiveled 360 degrees in her chair. Shopping had taken much less time than she'd expected. She had plenty of time to get ready now. Too much time, maybe. She didn't want to sit around, waiting for Hayes. It would really set her nerves on edge.

Violet eyed the computer screen. She *could* write some

fanfic. At the thought, a scene flashed into her head: a brightly lit football stadium, cheering fans, and Hayes, the high school quarterback, running onto the field.

No matter what, she'd tell him tonight that she was the fanfic writer. So what was the harm in one more installment? She began to type, the words flowing onto the screen like a fast-moving river.

"We are the Falcons. The mighty, mighty Falcons!" Franklin High cheerleaders led the crowd in a rousing cheer, then skipped off the field. The Franklin football team broke apart from a huddle. The time-out was over. It was the big homecoming game, and the score was 21–18, Falcons down by 3. There were seconds left in the second half.

"Go, Hayes!" the cheerleaders screamed. Hayes Grier, the quarterback, gave a slight bow to the girls, directing his gaze to one in particular—the new girl on the squad, Rose, who just happened to be Hayes's new girlfriend, too.

The Falcons got into position at the line of scrimmage. The Falcons had possession. Hayes stepped behind the crouching center, then called out the play: "29, 31, 5—hut!"

The center snapped the ball to Hayes. He caught it neatly. Then he stepped back, holding the ball high, looking to pass. The wide receivers weren't open, not one.

The clock was ticking. It was the last play of the game. What would Hayes do?

He feinted left, then ran right, out-maneuvering the opposition, player by player. Just as the buzzer sounded, he crossed into the end zone. Touchdown!

The crowd went crazy, chanting, "Hayes! Hayes! Hayes!" His teammates jumped on top of him, and they fell in a heap. Hayes pulled himself out of the pile, then trotted across the field. Everyone knew where he was going.

To Rose.

She stood at the side, a huge smile on her face. Hayes ran quicker and quicker, reached her, and swept her off her feet, twirling her around in a circle. He settled her back down, kissed her lightly on the lips, and whispered, "I was thinking of you the whole time. . . ."

The real Hayes Grier looked so handsome in his tux, Violet's heart hammered the entire limo ride to the red carpet. It barely registered she was sitting in her first limousine, a sleek black model that glistened in the starlight. She only had eyes for Hayes. "Wow!" he said when he saw her. "You clean up nice!"

Violet giggled. She thought she looked pretty good, too.

Not much later, they pulled into a long line of limos. They were there.

"Now," Hayes instructed, "when the driver reaches that spot in the front, someone will open the door for us. I'll get out first, then come back for you."

"Got it." Violet smiled nervously. She did get it—at least that part in the beginning. But it didn't mean she felt particularly comfortable stepping out of a limousine with high heels while paparazzi snapped pictures.

Before she knew it, the limousine stopped. The door swung open; Violet couldn't see who opened it. Hayes stepped out first.

"It's Hayes Grier!"

"Oh my God!"

"Hayes, I love you!"

Fans, standing behind velvet ropes, screamed again and again. Flashes popped, and reporters surged forward, holding out microphones. Hayes stepped closer to the fans, taking time to sign autographs and give high fives.

Then it was time for the press. "Hayes, over here! Hayes, tell us about your new movie! Hayes, give us a smile!"

Hayes grinned and waved, then reached back into the limo, holding out a hand to Violet. Violet took it, sidling out of the backseat, trying to smile.

"Who's your girlfriend?"

"What's your name, sweetheart?"

"Over here, look here!"

"Don't worry," Hayes whispered, slipping Violet's arm through his. "Just walk. When we get close to those reporters over there, in the press corral, you step to the side, and I'll talk to them. Then I'll get you, and we'll go inside."

"Okay." That sounded easy enough. Violet breathed a sigh of relief. The press wasn't really interested in her; they just wanted Hayes's attention. Maybe now she could enjoy herself.

Photographers snapped more pictures, and Violet walked slowly down the red carpet, feeling Hayes's body press against her side. When they reached the line of reporters, Hayes squeezed her arm, then went to talk to them one by one; each reporter wanted a few words with the newest teen star. Violet could hear Hayes fielding questions and answering easily.

He talked about *The Midnight Hawk*, about filming, and about Zan. Wait! Did she just hear her own name?

"Yes, my friend Violet," Hayes was saying, waving in her direction. "She's an intern at the studio. Isn't she great?" He posed for a picture, looking straight at Violet. Just as the camera flashed, he winked.

What did all that mean? Violet wondered. *He called me his friend, not his date. But then he winked. He's sending mixed signals, that's for sure.* She couldn't figure it out. Was he playing it safe because she pulled away from his kiss? Or did he just feel a deepening friendship? Nothing more?

And how did she really feel? Would she be okay with a friendship?

But all those questions could wait. The fanfic talk had to come first.

Hayes talked to the last reporter, then hurried to her side. "Ready, V?"

They walked into the reception area. Violet's heels sunk into the plush carpet. She gazed at the fancy tables set up around the room, the chandeliers hanging from the ceiling, and the groups of stylish people talking and laughing as they mingled. Was that Harry Lyons, from the boy band the Balloon Animals? And that had to be Belinda Faulkner at the table to the right, the star who put the Warrior Woman franchise on the map.

"Here we are," Hayes said, pulling out a chair for Violet. It was a table for two, and Violet sat down gratefully. Hayes moved the other chair next to hers and turned his back on the crowds.

Perfect, she thought. *Now is the time. I'll tell him I wrote those stories.*

"Having fun?" Hayes asked.

"It's amazing. I can't believe I'm here." She stopped herself from adding "with you." "But now that we have a few minutes to ourselves, I need to tell you—"

"Hayes!"

Violet closed her eyes and groaned. She recognized that voice immediately. It was T. J. Meyers. And he did not sound happy.

"Hayes!" TJ called again, making his way to the table, oblivious to everyone else there.

When he got closer, Violet saw his eyes were blazing and his expression contorted in rage. "I just heard something horrible."

TJ pulled a chair from the next table, right before a thin balding man was about to sit. Luckily, the man caught himself. He humphed loudly in TJ's direction. But TJ didn't notice.

"What is it?" Violet pictured a devastating fire burning down the set. Someone sick . . . or even dying.

"Jack Hunter—"

"Is he okay?" Hayes interrupted. Violet knew Jack Hunter was an assistant director, though she'd never spoken to him.

"He won't be when I get through with him," TJ said through gritted teeth. "He caused all those problems on the set yesterday. He's the reason we didn't have a stuntman!"

"Why?" Violet asked.

"He never booked a stuntman at all, that's why. And then he went and lied to me, saying he had. I'm leaving right now to fire him. Face-to-face. I want that satisfaction. I'll see you two tomorrow," he added, storming out of the room.

"Wow!" Hayes and Violet said at the same exact time. Hayes looked almost as upset as TJ.

"I can't believe Jack did that. That is definitely not cool."

Violet agreed. "Lucky you were able to step in," she said. "Otherwise, it would have delayed the whole production."

"Well, sure, there's that." Hayes nodded. "But lying is absolutely the worst, no matter the situation."

Violet's stomach dipped. She hadn't lied to Hayes, had she? It was more a sin of omission, of keeping something from him—even though she'd tried and tried to tell him.

"I can forgive just about anything," Hayes continued. "But lying? Forget it. For me, it's a deal breaker for any sort of relationship—friend, costar, boss, whatever."

Violet shifted in her seat.

"But don't get me started. I want you to have fun here! Let's pretend TJ never came over. You were starting to say something before?"

"Was I?" Violet said quickly. She couldn't tell him about the fanfic now, not when he was already so worked up about lying. "I can't remember!" she told him, adding another lie to the list.

How would she ever make things right?

———————

Violet tiptoed inside the Venice Beach house, turning to wave one last time to Hayes as he walked back to the limo. The rest of the night had passed in a blur. She remembered smiles and applause at the end of the movie, but nothing about the plot or the characters. And she must have talked to Hayes during the drive to Venice. For the life of her, though, she couldn't remember one thing she'd said.

From the bottom of the stairs, Violet could see that Mia was home. A line of light showed under her bedroom door. Violet smiled grimly and slowly started up the steps. Surely, Mia would have some advice to give or at least lend a sympathetic ear. Right now, she needed a friend.

"Mia," she said, softly knocking at the door. "Can I come in?"

Mia didn't answer.

Violet knocked again, louder, and opened the door slightly. Mia sat on her bed, sheets of paper spread around her, wearing headphones, nodding in time to the music.

She looked up, broke into a grin, and took off the headphones. "Hey, cuz! You look amazing. I heard you went to a premiere tonight."

So Uncle Forrest had paid attention!

"I'll tell you all about it later. But what's going on with you?" All of a sudden, Violet wanted to put off telling Mia about the night, just the way she'd been putting off talking to Hayes.

"Are you kidding? You go to a big-time premiere and walk the red carpet and I get to go first? All right, I'm just listening to the Balloon Animals for some design inspo."

"Well, you'll never guess who was at the premiere tonight—Harry Lyons!"

"No way. Okay, I'm done with recapping my night. Tell me all about it. It must have been awesome." Mia pushed aside the papers to make room. Violet kicked off her heels and flung herself on the bed. She gazed at the ceiling, not meeting Mia's eyes.

"I give it mixed reviews," Violet told her.

"You didn't like the movie?"

"I couldn't tell you one thing about the movie," Violet answered, rolling over onto her stomach. "I was talking about the whole night."

"Uh-oh. This doesn't sound good."

"I'll break it down for you. The limo ride and the red carpet get four stars—absolutely amazing. Everything that came after: zero stars. So that averages out to two. Like I said, mixed."

"What happened, exactly?"

Quickly, Violet explained how TJ came over and told them about the assistant director lying, and how Hayes went off on a rant, coming down hard on liars. "So I never got a chance to tell him about the fanfic. And now I'm not sure I ever can. He feels so strongly about lying, and I just waited too long. He'll never understand. He'll hate me." She grabbed a pillow and burrowed into it, facedown. "I don't want him to hate me."

"What? I can't hear you." Mia grabbed the pillow and tossed it onto the floor.

Violet turned her head, sighing. "I don't want him to hate me. I don't want to be that person to Hayes."

Mia leaned against the headboard, shaking her head. "I can't believe you didn't tell him."

"I know!" Violet wailed. "I should have told him yesterday. Or this morning. Or this afternoon when we were shopping. I haven't even told you about that, Mia! We had the best time."

Mia let her talk about the day, about the vibe she was getting from Hayes, but how she still wasn't sure how he really felt.

Finally, Mia cut in. "Okay, that's enough. We need to get back to tonight. You should have told Hayes as soon as TJ complained about that AD. It would have been the perfect time. The subject of lying was on the table, right there in the open for you to pick up and run with. If you had only said something then, Hayes wouldn't feel betrayed. But now . . ."

"But now what? What should I do?" Violet scooted

next to Mia. Her cousin always had strong opinions, always voiced her thoughts. Why was she holding back now?

"I don't know what to tell you," Mia finally answered. "You'll have to figure this one out on your own."

Violet closed her eyes, suddenly weary beyond belief. How could she figure anything out when she was more confused than ever?

CHAPTER THIRTEEN

AT THE STUDIO THE NEXT MORNING, Violet walked Zan, ran errands, and printed call sheets. She did everything she needed to, but she worked on autopilot, with half a mind. The other half was trying to figure out if she should tell Hayes the truth. It was one thing for him to be cool about fan fiction written by a stranger. It was another to have it written by a friend who'd kept it secret.

Violet handed the last sheet to the head of wardrobe, then came to a decision: She wouldn't decide. She'd wait to see Hayes and feel out the situation. If it seemed right, she'd explain everything. If it seemed wrong, she'd wait.

She glanced at her phone, noting the time. She should be meeting with Hayes in just a few minutes to go over his schedule for the afternoon. Right now he was on a soundstage, filming the laboratory scene where his dad held him prisoner.

The scene took place somewhere near the middle of the film: Hawk's dad tries to explain why he wants to use Hawk as a guinea pig—for the good of the human race, he claims.

Violet walked over to the set. "Are you here to see Hayes?" Derek the intern asked.

Violet nodded.

"Well, if I were you, I'd run the other way. He is not having a good day."

Suddenly, the set quieted. Filming had begun.

Violet edged closer to the action, peering around groups of people. Hayes and Byron James, the actor playing his father, stood between lab tables. Hayes was crying out, struggling to free himself from a force field his "dad" had rigged.

She heard Hayes say, "But you're my father. You took care of me. You went to all my soccer games. You bought me a puppy for my eighth birthday. How can you do this?"

"Cut!" TJ snapped. "Hayes, what are you doing? Your lines read, 'You took me to baseball games. You bought me my first baseball glove.' What gives?"

"I'm just trying to own the lines," Hayes said. "You know, make them more personal. I had to stick the puppy in."

Violet grinned. Of course he had to mention a dog!

"That is not acceptable!" TJ shouted. "Right now, you are not Hayes Grier. You are Hawk. And you need to say your lines exactly as they are written. It's really not that hard." He glared at Hayes. "Or is it?"

"No," Hayes mumbled, looking down at the floor.

"Good." TJ tugged at his spiky hair. "Everyone take a break to cool down. Let's call it lunch."

Really, Violet thought, TJ was the one who needed to cool down. He'd really gone ballistic.

"And you, the guy who's giving us some 'personal' spin on your character. Don't come back until you know your lines verbatim." TJ's eyes swept the cast and crew, daring them to challenge him. "And for those of you who don't know the definition of *verbatim*"—he settled on Hayes—"it means 'word for word.'"

TJ marched away, and an eerie quiet settled over the set. For a moment, everyone seemed frozen in place. Then, as if they'd all received a signal, they moved at the same time, hurrying in different directions.

Everyone except for Hayes.

He was still slumped between the lab tables, a crushed look on his face.

"Hayes?" Violet walked over, taking tentative steps. "You okay?" Her problems suddenly seemed insignificant. Hayes took precedence.

Hayes gazed at her and shook his head slightly. "So you saw that, too?"

"Yes, but it's not a big deal. TJ blows up at everybody, you know that. Once, I saw him shouting at a poor defenseless kitten who'd wandered onto the soundstage."

Hayes gave her a crooked grin. "You're kidding, right?"

"Maybe," Violet conceded, "but can't you see it happening? Really, Hayes, nobody thinks less of you for it."

Hayes shrugged. "I'm not sure about that." His grin faded, and his mouth turned down in disappointment. "I'm really mad at myself. I should have checked with TJ before I changed any lines. He likes to control every little thing during filming, and I know that."

"Do you need anything during the break?" Violet asked. "Iced coffee? A sandwich? A new director?"

Hayes laughed. "You always make me feel better, V. Can you come to my trailer and help with these lines so I can get them down"—he stressed the next word—"verbatim?"

Violet may have made Hayes feel better on set. But it seemed when they got to the trailer, Hayes was in an even deeper funk, patting Zan absentmindedly, moving listlessly, and refusing to eat anything.

"Let's take those lines from the top." Violet settled on the couch. She patted the cushion. "Come, sit down."

Obediently, Hayes sat.

"Do you want to read from the script?" she asked.

He shook his head. "I did memorize the lines earlier. You just check and see that I have every little word right."

Violet flipped through the pages until she got to the lab scene. "Hawk," she read as the father, "you have to understand this is for the greater good. These experiments will determine why you've survived on our planet. They could hold the key for extending human life."

"They could also kill me," Hayes said.

"True," Violet went on. "It is a bit of a sacrifice."

"Not on your part," Hayes said. "The only sacrifice is mine."

"Ahem." Violet coughed. "I'm the only sacrifice," she corrected gently.

"I'm the only sacrifice," Hayes repeated, his voice trembling a bit.

"I cared for you the best I could," Violet said, turning the page.

Hayes gave a strangled laugh. "You really had me fooled, Dad."

Violet nodded encouragingly.

"We really had some good times together," Hayes continued.

"Great," Violet interrupted. "Great times."

"Great times together." Hayes's voice grew weaker. "You took me to baseball games. You bought me my first glove."

"Baseball glove."

"Baseball glove! You're my dad. How can you ignore that?"

"How can you ignore *all* that."

"I give up!" Hayes stood and looked around wildly, as if searching for an escape route. "I'm flubbing all the lines, changing words, and it's not even on purpose!"

"Oh, Hayes." Violet gently pulled him back down to the couch. She didn't want him running off—or having any kind of breakdown on set. That would only make things worse with TJ.

"You're stressed, that's all." She held out his copy of the script. "Let's just read the dialogue out loud a few times before you try again. It's hard, I know. But you can do it. You've nailed other scenes before—longer, more complicated ones."

Hayes nodded, looking a little calmer. He took the pages. "I'll read them to myself a couple of times first, just to get them down."

While Hayes scanned the pages, Violet let her mind wander back to her own dilemma: when to tell Hayes that she wrote the fanfic. It was no longer a question of "if." She was wrong to keep it from him, wrong to have done it in the first place, to create secret "Hayes Grier" stories about him when they had a relationship. It turned the fiction into lies, giving him a personal life he might not like at all.

Violet could see that now. When she was writing, she was too caught up in the emotion and the story, but taking a step back, she wished she'd never started.

Now, more than ever, Violet wanted to tell him. She could feel the words on the tip of her tongue, trying to escape, to clear her conscience and set the record straight.

She looked at Hayes, so vulnerable, his head bent over the script.

But she couldn't tell him now, not when he was already so distraught. Not when he had to get those lines down in—she glanced at the clock—thirty minutes. It wouldn't be fair.

Of course, the longer she waited the more it would hurt their relationship. But that wasn't important now. Hayes needed to concentrate on his role. He needed her support.

"Ready?" she asked.

Hayes nodded.

"Hawk," she began, "you have to understand . . ."

Ten minutes later, she put down the script. "Perfect!" she told Hayes. "Now let's show TJ!"

———————

Hayes was going to makeup for a touch-up before the shoot. So Violet took her time in the trailer, straightening up and playing with Zan. She was heading toward the laboratory set to watch the filming when she heard her name.

"Hey, wait up!" Coco caught up to Violet. "I heard TJ really chewed out Hayes." She shook her head sympathetically. "I really feel for the guy."

Violet felt so drained, she couldn't quite focus on Coco. She blinked and looked away.

"Violet?" Coco reached for her arm. "Are you okay? You seem upset. Is it TJ? Did something happen with you, too?"

Violet shook her head, tears unexpectedly springing to her eyes.

"Well, then what's wrong?"

"Nothing." Violet tried to smile. Violet liked Coco. She believed Coco really wanted to help. But she couldn't tell her about the stories, about Hayes hating liars, or her feelings for Hayes. Except for Mia, no one knew her secret. And no one could know, until she told Hayes.

"Allergies. I forgot to take my allergy pill this morning, so everything is really getting to me."

Coco looked at her skeptically. "Well, for what it's worth, TJ has been on a rampage all day. It's not you, Violet. It's him."

Violet almost laughed. It's what she'd been trying to tell Hayes.

"Don't take it personally," Coco continued, linking her arm through Violet's.

"Thanks, Coco," Violet said. The girl really was trying to make her feel better. She couldn't know that her problems had nothing to do with TJ. "I feel better now."

Coco tilted her head, peering closely at Violet. "I don't believe you," she declared. "But whatever's wrong, I have the cure. A girls' night out on the town. And I won't take no for an answer."

Violet just wanted to go home and crawl into bed after work. But she could tell Coco meant what she said, and it would take as much energy to resist as it would to go out.

She nodded.

"Good!" said Coco. "What time should I pick you up?"

"Here we are!" Coco parked her car by the VALET sign, tossed the keys to an attendant, and led Violet to the door of Sing It, Sister!

"What kind of place is this?"

"It's a karaoke bar. We get to sing along with our favorite tunes, and the audience gets to go crazy for us."

Singing in public? That would certainly be different, Violet thought. "Well, I like the name."

Coco patted her shoulder as they walked inside. "I wasn't kidding about girls' night out, Violet. Tonight is all about sisterhood. We're going to have a blast!"

People streamed in behind them, and Violet saw the place was already packed. Sing It, Sister! was definitely the place to be. Bright lights lit a large stage; neon-shaped guitars, microphones, and musical notes hung on every wall. Music blared, and Violet nodded her head to the beat.

This spot could be the Times Square of LA, Violet thought. *You hang around long enough, you'll see everyone you know.* She grinned at Coco.

Coco grinned back. "I told you. It's the ultimate cure for the blues."

Coco found an empty spot by a wall, and the girls squeezed in. They gazed at the stage. Two guys in their twenties bounced around to an old Beatles song, reading the lyrics from a screen. The audience clapped along.

The guys wore hip-looking suits, and probably came straight from work to blow off steam. That's what she wanted to do, Violet thought. Blow off steam.

Coco nudged her. "So," she said, waving at the stage. "Shall we?"

Violet was definitely ready. "What are we waiting for?" She grabbed Coco's hand and pulled her into the crowd.

"Whoa!" Coco laughed. "We have to sign up first and wait our turn. Just give me a sec." She reached for her phone, buzzing with messages. "Ugh! So many. Listen, you go choose a song, put us on the list, and I'll read through some of these texts."

Violet threaded through the crowd, found the songbook on the corner of the bar, and flipped through the pages. There were hundreds of songs, maybe thousands. She paused at a section marked "Girl Groups." She could find something here, something empowering, Violet thought. Something for sisterhood! But even under that one listing, the song titles went on and on . . .

"Hey, can somebody else get a look at that?" a woman said behind her.

"Sorry!" Violet quickly decided on a song called "Standing Together, Never Alone." She scribbled her and Coco's names on a sheet and made her way back.

Coco was still holding her phone, scrolling through the screen. "Oh my God," she said. "I've never gotten so many texts at one time. I'm sorry, Violet, but I've got to go. TJ needs to meet with Hayes and me. He's called an emergency dinner meeting. We have to go over that last scene. He says it's mandatory."

"It's okay. Go, go!" Violet pushed her toward the door. The last thing she wanted to do was make TJ mad. "I know things have been crazy on set. And that scene is so important!"

"Thanks for understanding!" Coco gave her a quick

hug. "And I promise. We're going to do this again. And next time"—she pointed to the stage—"we'll be stars!"

Coco turned away, shouting, "Excuse me, pardon me," over the music, shouldering through the next wave of partiers coming in.

Suddenly, in a room full of people, Violet felt alone. She put in an Uber request on her phone. Ten minutes. She'd wait and watch the singers, then leave.

She gazed at the stage. A woman with wavy dark hair was just stepping off the stage. The emcee leaped up, grabbing the mic. "I'm back," he told the audience. "And it looks like our next singers are a duo—who will be singing 'Standing Together, Never Alone.'" He paused, looking at the list. "Violet and Coco, come on up!"

Violet groaned. She'd chosen a long slow song, a soulful ballad, thinking she and Coco could pull it off together. Now what?

The crowd quieted as everyone looked for the singers. "Coco?" people whispered. "Is she really here?"

Another mistake! Why did Violet use Coco's real name? She should have made something up!

"Hey," shouted the woman who had been behind her at the bar. Heads turned as she pointed to Violet. "You're not Coco, but aren't you . . . Violet?"

Before Violet could answer, the emcee shouted, "Here she is! One part of the duo! Violet!"

People started to clap encouragingly. They parted, leaving an open path to the stage.

The emcee shielded his eyes from the lights and called, "Don't be shy! We're all friends here."

Violet looked back at the door, blocked by the dense throng. Would it be easier to just go onstage and get it over with?

Not knowing what else to do, Violet slowly walked forward. The emcee leaned over and held out a hand to help her up. Onstage, she couldn't see a thing; the audience was lost in the lights. She glanced back at the emcee, who was disappearing through a door at the back of the stage.

The music started. She gripped the mic. She couldn't sing! She thought she might be able to, but she just couldn't. Instead, she said in a squeaky voice, "Coco and I were supposed to stand together." She stopped, then added, "And now I'm alone. Got to go!"

She dropped the mic. It clattered to the floor, a screeching sound filling the room. She ran to the back door and slipped off the stage.

"Huh?" said a man wearing a white apron, his hair pulled back in a net. Violet was in the kitchen. The chef looked at her curiously.

"How do I get out of here?" she asked in a panic. He pointed behind him. "Thank you!" she called. Racing around refrigerators and counters, she found another door marked EXIT. She raced through and found herself in a dark alley. She made her way to the street.

Now where was that Uber?

Violet pushed open the front door. Well, she was back home, that was good. But she felt even worse than before she'd left. The night was a fiasco. Going onstage, then running away? How ridiculous was that? But it did take her mind off her Hayes dilemma, that was for sure.

"Violet!" Mia rushed over, pulling Violet inside. She breathlessly slammed the door behind her. "I can't believe it!"

"Can't believe what?"

"Have you seen it?"

"Seen what?" Violet was losing patience.

"The picture of Hayes and Coco."

"Oh." Violet walked into the kitchen to get a glass of water. Her throat felt dry and scratchy, even though she hadn't sung a note. "I know they're together tonight. It's not a big deal, Mia. Calm down. Coco had to leave the karaoke bar for an emergency meeting with Hayes and TJ."

"Just look!" Mia stepped in front of her and practically shoved the phone in her face. Violet squinted. The photo was on Newsflash!, a celebrity gossip site, and it was dated that night, just an hour ago. The picture was dark and grainy, but its subjects were unmistakably Hayes and Coco.

They were kissing.

And TJ was nowhere in sight.

Violet felt like she'd been hit by a train. *I've been betrayed,* she thought—*by Coco, and by Hayes!*

CHAPTER FOURTEEN

ANOTHER NIGHT AND, ONCE AGAIN, Violet hardly slept at all. This was getting to be a habit, and Violet didn't like it. Early the next morning, she examined her face in the mirror: Puffy eyelids. Circles under the eyes. A haggard look. Turning away, she pulled her hair back in a ponytail without checking to see how it looked. She should really look her best for work. But at this point, she thought, it didn't really matter.

Violet grabbed her backpack from the hall and had just reached the front door when her phone buzzed. She paused, wanting to ignore it. Really, she just wanted the world to go away. Of course, she couldn't, though, looking at her phone was a knee-jerk reaction. She swiped the screen.

"Oh!" Violet yelped. The message was from the fanfic website, but it wasn't from an ordinary reader. It was from Lydia Jacobs.

Hello? the message began. *Are you there, mystery writer? I still want to meet you. ASAP. I can guarantee you ten meetings in one week, starting with the head of A-List Studios and ending with director Zoe Zalewski. Everyone— and I mean everyone—is freaking out over your fanfic. It's awesome. So get in touch—now!*

Now this is how to beat the blues, Violet thought. For a moment she forgot about Coco and Hayes. She forgot that the fanfic could be trouble. This was her big break. Nothing would stop her now!

She opened her mouth wide and sang some lines from the karaoke song, changing up the words: "I'm standing with Lydia Jacobs. I'm not alone, don't you know!"

Violet skipped down to the driveway and stopped short. The garage was empty. Apparently something could stop her: lack of a car.

"Anything wrong?"

Violet jumped. She spun around, then smiled. "Oh, hi, Jay. I was about to drive to work. But my uncle must have taken the car."

Violet's mind raced. Did she leave anything she needed

in the car? Going by her recent luck, the answer had to be a resounding yes. Frantically, she searched through her backpack.

Jay smiled at her. "You have a hard time in the mornings, don't you?" He spoke in a teasing way, like he actually found that appealing.

"Oh, you catch me at my worst, when I'm running late. I'll call an Uber."

"Don't be silly. You don't know how long that will take. I can drive you."

He was being so nice. How could Violet refuse?

Jay drove a Volvo SUV. Her parents would be pleased, Violet thought. The car had a high safety rating, and Jay took the curves with a sure, steady hand. She leaned back against the seat and tried to relax.

Jay glanced over. Violet knew he was noting her strained, haggard look and her toes anxiously tapping the car mat. It turned out she couldn't forget about the fanfic. Lydia Jacobs's offer meant her name would come out. Everyone would know Violet Reeves was HollywoodWriter310. Even Hayes.

"It's not just getting to work on time," he said. "Is it? Something else is wrong."

"No," she insisted. "It's nothing, really."

"Why don't you tell me, Violet? I want to help."

Violet sank deeper into the seat and sighed. She couldn't tell him everything, of course. She couldn't admit to her feelings for Hayes or that Hayes and Coco had kissed. She couldn't even talk about the fanfic. But she could give him a general idea of one problem: Lydia Jacobs. If only she'd talked to Hayes earlier, she could meet with Lydia with a clear conscience. But, with Hayes still in the dark, it didn't feel right—even if he was with Coco now.

Jay seemed like a totally nice, totally together guy. And he must be smart. Maybe he really could help.

"Okay," she agreed. "What would you do if you were handed a dream opportunity? But if you took that opportunity, you'd wind up hurting somebody you cared about?"

Luckily, Jay didn't press for details. He drove for a bit, thinking, then said, "This is my take on it. Ready?"

"Ready."

"You should be honest with the person you care about. If the opportunity is really your dream, this person— with time—will understand. He or she may be hurt, but eventually, they'll come around. That is," he stressed, "as long as you're honest."

Violet nodded, gazing out the car window quietly until they reached the studio. The guard caught Violet's eye and waved them in, and Jay pulled over by the soundstage. "So," he said, "what do you think?"

"I think you may be right." She smiled and patted his hand. "Thanks for the ride, Jay, and for the good advice."

She opened the door to leave.

"Wait!" Jay said. "There's a beach party tonight in Venice. Why don't you come? It will take your mind off things."

Violet had tried that strategy before—at Sing It, Sister!— and it hadn't worked that way at all. But it did sound like a nice night out. Maybe she deserved a break. She caught a glimpse of her tired-looking reflection in the window. But maybe she'd be so zonked out, all she'd want to do is sleep.

"I'm not sure I'll be up for it," she told him honestly. "Can I text you later?"

They exchanged numbers. Violet stepped out of the car and called as he pulled away, "I'll let you know!"

Now, she thought, *I just have to get through the day.*

As usual, the set was a blur of motion: tech people setting up lights and cameras, cast members rushing to makeup and wardrobe. Violet spied Hayes by the craft service table, munching on a chocolate chip muffin.

A big piece fell on the floor. Hayes quickly bent to pick it up, popping it in his mouth, then looking around to see if anyone had noticed. It was so little-boy cute, it just about broke Violet's heart.

Stop it, she told herself sternly.

The key to surviving the workday, she thought, was to put aside her feelings. Forget about Hayes and Coco. Remember Hayes was the movie's star, and her job was to keep him on-target.

"Hey," she said, checking the schedule. "You're due for a photo shoot soon for the new movie poster."

"Morning, V," Hayes said, reaching for a napkin. "You're all business this morning! Sorry your night out with Coco was cut short."

So you two could hook up, Violet couldn't help but think. But it was weird. Hayes was acting like his usual normal self, like last night didn't happen at all.

"Cheer up!" he said, moving closer to tap her shoulder. "You guys can get together another time."

So he thought she was upset because Coco had left the karaoke bar? Not because he'd kissed her.

So what did Hayes think of their relationship, then? His and Violet's? Of course, they weren't boyfriend/girlfriend. So he really had every right to kiss another girl. But they did have something. A certain connection, a special one. She could see it in his eyes and feel it in her heart every time they spoke. Even now, when she wanted to run away from him, she felt a pull to hold his hand, to stroke his cheek. Chemistry, plain and simple.

So much for putting aside her feelings.

"How was your dinner meeting?" Violet asked, striving to sound like she was making small talk.

"Nothing special." Hayes shrugged. "We went over that final scene and talked it through. It turned out to be an early night. TJ wanted us to get some rest."

Inside, Violet fumed. So the dinner was nothing special? They just worked? Hayes must think she lived in a world without Internet. And now he was lying! The guy who claimed he hated dishonesty! He was keeping the truth from her . . . unless he didn't think his new "relationship" should be her concern. Maybe he thought he and Violet weren't even friends, just boss and assistant!

Could she have been completely off on this? Were all these feelings one-sided?

Violet was taking Zan back to the trailer. She'd let him run around a back lot with benches and a playground. He'd played for an hour, fetching an old tennis ball. Each time he brought it back, she'd say, "You're a good dog! You're not like your owner at all, are you, boy?"

"Hi, Violet!" Coco was walking in the same direction. She motioned to her phone, meaning she was on a call. "We'll talk later," she whispered, one hand covering the receiver.

Violet nodded curtly, then sped up so they wouldn't walk in step. Behind her, she could hear Coco laughing. "I know!" she said to whomever she was talking to. "I think it's really going to work out. Last night was so great."

Quickly, Violet veered off to the side. She found a quiet spot behind another trailer. She leaned against the side, then sank to the ground. That was it. Proof that Coco and Hayes were an item. And where did that leave her?

Crying at work.

She let a few tears trickle down her cheeks. It felt good to release the emotion. But the next minute, she stood, drying her cheeks with her sleeve. She had to get herself under control. She was on set! She walked back around the trailer and saw Coco had stopped, too. She was leaning against a lamppost, the phone against her ear, still chatting happily. She couldn't escape that girl!

Of course, it wasn't Coco's fault; Violet knew that. Coco had no idea how Violet felt. Violet liked Coco; she really did. But now they wouldn't ever be friends. And what about Hayes? Maybe he wasn't totally at fault, either. Maybe he felt just as confused as she did.

"Hey, V. What's up?" Hayes was loping toward her, his step easy, his face set in a friendly, open way. Violet froze, not saying a word. Hayes didn't seem to notice. He kept walking. "Hey, Coco," he said in exactly the same way.

"Thank you again for last night, Hayes!" Coco called out in a flirty sort of voice.

That did it! Instantly, Violet felt a shift. She was angry

now, not sad or confused; she actually stamped her foot. She'd show them both. She pulled out her phone, tapped on Jay's contact info, and began to text: *If your invitation still stands, I'd love to come to that beach party.*

The sun was setting over the water. The sky, a rainbow of colors, looked so beautiful, it seemed more like a painting. For a moment, Violet just stood on the boardwalk, admiring the view.

"Come on," Mia said, tugging her hand. "The party's already started."

"Thank God you're here," Violet told her cousin as they stepped onto the sand. "I won't know anyone here but Jay."

"Well, I'm guessing he'll only be talking to you, anyway," Mia teased. "I think the boy has got it bad."

Violet elbowed her. "Stop it! You don't know that."

But sure enough, Jay was already coming over, a huge grin on his face. "Hi, Violet. Hi, Mia." He hugged Violet tight and whispered, "I'm so glad to see you."

Maybe Mia was right. Violet felt pleased. Finally, a guy who made his feelings clear.

Jay waved over to a group of people piling driftwood into the center of a circle of beach chairs and blankets. "I'll introduce you."

He took Violet's hand and led her to the group. "Everyone!" he called out. "This is Violet." He pointed to friends, naming them one by one. Violet tried to remember who was who. There was a boy-Dylan and a girl-Dylan, and twins named Isabel and Jacob, but she soon lost track. Everyone smiled and waved, but Jay seemed content to keep her to himself. Mia, meanwhile, wandered off to join some girls wading into the water.

Someone lit a fire. Bit by bit the flames grew bigger, until it was a full-fledged bonfire. Violet and Jay found a spot in the circle and sat close together.

By now, the sky had darkened. Stars blinked brightly. The fire crackled, sending sparks into the air. A guy with long, straight hair strummed a guitar.

It was a perfect night; couples leaned close to one another, caught up in the romance of the evening. Violet pushed thoughts of Hayes out of her mind. She was here with Jay—sweet, smart Jay—who really liked her. She was determined to like him back.

One of the Dylans passed them sticks and marshmallows to make s'mores, along with chocolate bars and graham crackers.

"That's s'more like it," Violet joked, thinking that was something Hayes and his squad would say. Jay didn't seem to hear. *Just as well,* she thought. *It was pretty lame.*

Violet and Jay edged closer to the fire to hold their

marshmallows over the flames. When the marshmallows turned golden brown, they pushed them onto a cracker, adding the chocolate and another cracker. "My favorite sandwich," Violet said, taking a big bite.

"Plain, simple, and delicious," Jay agreed.

"I don't know, I like my desserts on the weird side," Violet went on. "The stranger the better. One time I made a s'more with peanut butter, cinnamon, maple syrup, and sprinkles."

Jay twisted his face. "Ew. That is weird. Did you actually eat it?"

"Of course I ate it. That was the point!"

Jay nodded, but Violet knew he didn't get it. And it bothered her. Why did crazy ingredients make such a difference to her? Violet wasn't sure. Maybe it had to do with individuality and a sense of adventure.

Hayes had gotten it right away. He got her, in fact. There was that almost-instant bond, a spark that seemed to be missing with Jay.

But maybe Violet wasn't being fair. *Open mind, Violet,* she told herself. *Open mind.* She finished the s'more, licked her fingers, and smiled at Jay.

A cool breeze ruffled her hair.

Immediately, Jay took off his sweatshirt and draped it around Violet's shoulders, keeping his arm around her. "Better?" he asked.

"Better," she said, snuggling closer. Jay cupped her chin and tilted his face, moving nearer and nearer for a kiss. Violet closed her eyes and parted her lips, letting it happen. They pressed against each other, and Violet felt . . .

Nothing.

She opened her eyes and pulled back. Someone called Jay over. He looked at her questioningly, and she nodded, giving him permission to go. Alone, she stared into the fire, knowing her feelings once and for all.

She wasn't into Jay. No matter how hard she tried, she couldn't force the attraction. The bottom line: She was using him to take her mind off Hayes and to make herself feel better. That wasn't right.

Hayes . . . now she knew her true feelings for him, too. It had been building since the moment they met, with some setbacks, of course, while she figured things out. She didn't want a friendship. She'd fallen for him—hard. And one way or another, she had to see it through.

She knew it may already be too late. He could very well be with Coco now. And who knew how he would react when he found out about the fan fiction.

There were so many "what ifs," Violet felt like her head was spinning.

But one thing was for sure. She needed to leave the party. She couldn't keep leading on Jay. Quickly she found Mia and said, "We need to go."

"What do you mean? What about Jay?"

Violet's eyes swept the beach, the bonfire, and the water. She didn't see him anywhere. She'd have to talk to him later and explain it all. It wasn't ideal, but right now she'd have to text.

Quickly, she typed, *I'm sorry. Had to go.* And they left.

CHAPTER FIFTEEN

THE NEXT MORNING AT THE STUDIO, Violet peered into the editing room. Hayes was going over some film with the editor, watching a scene from the day before. Violet nodded. He was right where he was supposed to be. On schedule.

Just looking at his serious expression, his lean body tucked into a chair, made Violet's cheeks flush. Wow! Was it going to be like this all the time? Now that she'd pinned down her feelings, would her heart hammer in her chest every time she saw him? Quietly, she backed away.

She was in such a state, and she hadn't even spoken to him yet. How could she ask about Coco? How could she explain about the fanfic? She knew she had to now, more than ever. But it was all too much. She had no idea where to start.

Just then Violet's phone buzzed with a text from Hayes: *Leaving editing. Let's meet in my trailer to go over my schedule ASAP. And you have to help me prep. That big emotional scene is tomorrow!*

Violet stared at the screen. He had no idea she was right down the hall. And she wanted to keep it that way until she got her act together. She had a new goal: to know where Hayes was every second of the day. So she could avoid him.

"Okay, see you later," she heard him say to the film editor.

Starting right now!

Violet hurried into the first empty office she saw. She hid behind the open door, pressing against the wall until he passed.

Only then did she text back: *Busy now!* She closed the screen, leaving it at that.

Suddenly, footsteps sounded closer. Someone was coming! The door swung closed, leaving her in full view.

The man jumped back, startled. "Who are you?"

"N-n-n-nobody," Violet stuttered. "Just an intern. I may be lost. This isn't T. J. Meyers's office?"

"No," the man said, "it's mine. I think he's in the next building over."

"Thanks so much!" Violet said, rushing away.

She spent the rest of the morning pretending to be absorbed in paperwork, taking notes on production changes and offering her services to everyone except Hayes.

She was just picking up dry cleaning for Marion Lewis, the actress who was playing Hayes's mom, when TJ stopped her.

"There you are!" he said, annoyed. "Hayes has been looking for you all morning. Haven't you gotten his texts?"

Violet shook her head, crossing her fingers behind her back. She'd put her phone on silent and hadn't so much as peeked at her messages. "I must be out of power."

She was piling on the lies now. She didn't like it. It made her feel awful, like she wasn't the person she thought she was. It had to stop, and it would—as soon as she figured out how to talk to Hayes.

"The final scene shoots tomorrow," TJ was telling her. "He needs you to help him. You know he's having trouble with the emotional end of it."

"I do know, but isn't there somewhere else I'm needed more? Maybe another actor should go over the lines with Hayes, someone who can give more guidance."

"You're his assistant," TJ said testily. "He wants you. Now."

"A coffee run?" Violet continued as if she hadn't heard. "Lunch orders? Dry cleaning pickup?"

TJ rolled his eyes and walked away, not saying a word.

In Hayes's trailer, Violet perched awkwardly on the edge of a chair. The seat was by the door, as far from Hayes and the couch as she could get.

Hayes looked at her, puzzled. "You seem like you're ready to run away."

"Ha!" Violet barked out a laugh. "I'm just gearing up for the scene."

"Okay. I'm a little tense, too." Hayes ran his fingers through his hair nervously. "This scene is really hard for me."

Violet's heart went out to him. She wanted to help him. But it was just so difficult being here with him, not saying anything and feeling so awkward. He was right; she really did want to run out the door. She had forced herself to come, knowing if she hadn't TJ would find out, and once again her job would be on the line. One of these days, he'd ask about the new script she was writing. The script she hadn't started. She didn't want him annoyed at her already for messing up with Hayes.

"Okay, let's go through the beginning lines, when Coco—I mean Devon—thinks she's still running away with you."

Hayes flipped through pages of the script, stopping near the end. "I'll start with just a read. Ready?"

"Ready."

"You don't sound ready."

"Just go ahead," Violet managed to say.

"Are you cold, Devon?" Hayes read out loud.

"A little. I packed in such a hurry, I didn't bring a jacket."

"Here, take mine . . ."

They went through the lines. "Now I'll do it for real." Hayes stood up. "This is the hard part now."

"What?" Violet looked up at him blankly. "What are we doing again?"

"V!" Hayes strode over to her chair. "You're so out of it! What's wrong?"

This should have been her cue, her time to blurt out the whole fan-fiction story. Talk about her feelings and ask about that kiss with Coco. Somehow, though, she couldn't bring herself to do it.

She tried to tell herself she was thinking of Hayes, that it wasn't fair to burden him with all this while he was working on the scene. And that was part of it. But mostly—she had to admit—she was chicken. She wanted her confession to be letter perfect. If she spoke now, she'd burst into tears and wouldn't be able to talk, let alone speak coherently. Right now, she just couldn't deal. And she had time. She wasn't going to get back to Lydia and reveal her identity until this whole thing was straightened out with Hayes.

Hayes tossed the script on the coffee table. "This isn't doing either of us any good. We need to clear our minds. We need a change of scenery."

"We do?" Violet said weakly.

"Definitely." He pulled her to her feet. "I know exactly what will cheer you up."

"You do?" Violet didn't actually doubt that Hayes did know; knew exactly, in fact, what would make her laugh and what would make her cry.

"I'm going to get you out of here, and show you something amazing. It's a special place." Hayes grinned widely and his shoulders relaxed. "I won't tell you now, but it's really close to my heart."

He opened the door and gave a goofy little bow. "After you!"

Violet paused, torn in two directions. She felt her body move toward him willingly, happily, of its own accord. She wanted to go, of course she did! They'd be together, away from the studio and its pressures, just the two of them. But would it be like before, when they went shopping? Before Coco? So much had happened since, and the feelings overwhelmed her.

Her phone buzzed, and she looked at the message from TJ: *Are you with our boy? Please confirm.*

That decided it. She had to go. *Yes*, she texted. *For the rest of the day.*

"So this is your special place!" Violet stood outside the door to Dogtown Dog Shelter, her hands on her hips. Really, she should have guessed. Their driver said something about "Zan" and "the usual" and knew exactly where to go. Like every Hayes Grier fan, Violet knew Hayes had adopted Zan from an animal shelter.

As soon as they walked inside, a tall woman hurried over. Her name tag read ANNIE TRENT, DIRECTOR. "Hayes!" she exclaimed. "This is a surprise. You're not scheduled to come in until tomorrow."

"I know, but my friend Violet and I needed to see some friendly faces."

Annie laughed. "You mean mine or the dogs'?"

"Both!"

"Welcome, Violet." Annie extended her hand to shake. "Any friend of Hayes's is a friend to the shelter."

The word *friend* repeated again and again and again caused Violet's throat to tighten. Was any other relationship just hopeless?

"Hello," she said, trying to smile. "It's nice to meet you."

"You know the drill, Hayes," Annie went on. "Violet needs to fill out some forms, and then you're good to go. And remember, don't bother signing in. We don't want word to get out you volunteer here every week!"

As Violet penciled in her information, she peered at Hayes sitting next to her on a couch. "So you come here every week?"

Hayes shrugged. "As often as I can. Sometimes it's tough

to get away. But I try my best. This place keeps me grounded. It reminds me what's important."

Violet gazed across the lobby, watching a little boy leave with his dad, an adorable black puppy yapping at his heels.

"That's so cute," she said. "It's great that that puppy is getting a home."

"That little guy reminds me of Zan." Hayes snapped a photo on his phone. He blushed a bit. "I like to show Zan pictures when I get back."

A young girl and her mom walked in the door next and went to talk to Annie about adopting an older dog. The girl, about twelve, Violet guessed, kept glancing at Hayes. Hayes noticed, gave her a smile, but shifted so his back was to her. Then he put on a baseball cap, turning down the brim.

"I hope she doesn't recognize me. I'm trying to keep this volunteering gig quiet. No Vine, Snapchat, or Instagram."

Violet thought about the publicist and how thrilled she would be to discover all these photo ops. "I get it," she said. "You want your privacy."

"It's more than that," Hayes told her. "I mean, I love my fans, and I want to connect with them. But if they knew I worked here, they might sign up too in the hopes of meeting me. And that's just plain wrong. They should come to help the dogs. If they're donating their time, it should be for the right reasons."

"Oh." Violet felt a lump form in her throat. Hayes was

really so kind and generous. She was struck once again by how much he cared. Did he care about her in that same general way? Was he trying to cheer her up, because that's just the kind of guy he was, and he would do the same for anybody? Or did it mean something more?

And if Coco was feeling down, would she be here in Violet's place?

Violet signed the last form and stood. "Let's get going," she told Hayes, leaving the papers on the front desk. Hayes pushed open a side door, and they entered a cavernous space. Little rooms lined the sides, a half-door gate in front of each. Dogs jumped up and down in each one, yipping and yapping at the sight of Hayes and Violet.

Violet covered her ears and looked beseechingly at Hayes. The dogs were cute—all sizes and colors—but the noise was almost overwhelming.

"They'll settle down," Hayes promised. "Just give them a minute. In the meantime, let's put on gloves and grab some equipment."

"Gloves? Equipment? What does that mean exactly?"

"It means we'll be doing some cleaning, V." Hayes laughed as she wrinkled her nose, peering at the dog droppings spread out on the kennel floors. "It's all part of the job. If we have time, we can bring the dogs outside in the run. But this comes first."

They went to a big, walk-in closet to get ready. By

the time they came back out—pooper-scoopers in gloved hands—the dogs had indeed quieted down.

"Do we get to work together?" Violet asked. Somehow, the idea of picking up poop didn't seem so terrible if she could do it with Hayes.

"Well, I usually work alone . . ." Hayes grinned at her and gave her a playful push. "But I'll make an exception just this once."

He reached inside one gate and held the dog back while they slipped inside. "This is Arnold," he said, scratching the giant dog behind his ears. "I think he's a mix of German shepherd and retriever. But I'm just guessing."

Arnold, thumping his tail, looked at Violet. She patted him on the head, just as Hayes reached to do the same. Their fingers brushed. An electric shock ran through Violet's body. She and Hayes looked at each other over Arnold's head, and the moment seemed frozen in time.

Hayes cleared his throat. "Let's take care of this, then we'll come back with a hose to wash down the floor."

"Is Arnold really the only dog in this room?" Violet leaned over to pick up one of the droppings.

"Yes, but he's got a big appetite."

While they worked, Arnold raced around them like an excited puppy, and Violet forgave him for his messes. Then Hayes ushered Arnold through a door at the back of the room into an enclosed outdoor space.

Hayes closed the door behind him and told Violet, "Now we get the hoses."

As they dragged the hoses into the room, Violet gazed at the back of Hayes's head with mixed feelings.

There'd been long moments when she'd forgotten about Coco and just enjoyed being with Hayes. But then she'd come to her senses with a jolt, realizing she couldn't ignore the kiss. In fact, her emotions were coming to a boil. She couldn't hold back her questions any longer.

Hayes lifted the doggy bed, water bowl, and food dish onto a shelf, and they switched on the hoses. They each doused a corner. Her back to Hayes, Violet blurted, "I saw you kissing Coco!"

"What?" Hayes spun toward Violet, and the stream of water drenched her shoes. Surprised, she jumped back, and her hose struck Hayes full in the chest. They both dropped the hoses as if they were hot potatoes. The hoses writhed on the floor like slithering snakes, spraying every which way.

"Turn them off!" Hayes shouted.

They ran after the hoses, bumping into each other, slipping in puddles. A second later, they both went down. They fell on top of each other, giggling and laughing, getting wetter and wetter until they could reach the nozzles to shut down the streams.

Violet's giggles trailed off. Hayes sighed. They lay on the

cool wet floor, side by side, catching their breath and staring up at the ceiling.

"That was really something," Hayes finally said.

"I know. I feel like I've been through a wash cycle."

"No, I mean about what you said. About me kissing Coco."

"Oh." Violet turned her head, the same time Hayes did. Their noses were an inch apart. She gazed down at Hayes's T-shirt, stuck to his skin. She could see every muscle, each ab outlined as if he were a Greek god, sculpted as a statue. She caught her breath.

Hoping her shirt wasn't quite as revealing, she tugged a bit at the bottom.

"You actually saw us kissing?"

"No," Violet admitted. "Mia showed me a picture from some website."

Hayes inched closer so their noses touched. "So that's what's bothering you?"

Violet nodded, and their noses rubbed. Her stomach dipped.

"Nothing is going on between Coco and me," Hayes said in a whisper. "It wasn't even a real kiss. We posed for a photographer that way on purpose. Coco is in love with some other guy. She wanted to make him jealous, so she asked me to kiss her in front of the camera. And you know me," Hayes half-joked. "I can never turn down a friend."

"*Do* I know you?" Violet murmured.

"You should know I'd never do anything to hurt you. I'm so sorry, V. But our whole relationship is confusing. I didn't think you cared, after we had that thing at the Hollywood Sign. That's why I didn't mention the paparazzi photo. I didn't think you felt the same way about me as I do about you."

"I do," she whispered, so softly she wasn't sure she'd spoken aloud.

She must have, though, for slowly, slowly, Hayes drew Violet closer, so their bodies touched head to toe. At the same instant, they closed their eyes.

This is it, Violet thought. *Our first kiss.*

Suddenly the back door swung open and Arnold rushed in, jumping between the two, barking furiously.

Violet and Hayes laughed uncontrollably. "We'll get back to that later," Hayes told her. He eyed the room, water still funneling down the sloping ground into a drain. "But let's finish up here and see if we can find some dry clothes to borrow."

CHAPTER SIXTEEN

VIOLET LET HERSELF INTO THE VENICE HOUSE, feeling like she was walking on air. *What a difference a few hours can make*, she thought, smiling. She didn't want to use the word *love*—it was way too early for that. But this feeling that swept her from head to toe must be pretty darn close. She heard the sound of rattling dishes coming from the kitchen.

"Mia?" she called. "Is that you?"

"Live and in person," Mia called. "Come talk to me."

Violet walked in, and Mia, standing by the sink, did a double take. "What on earth are you wearing?" she asked.

Violet grinned. "What, you didn't see this very same outfit on the cover of *Vogue*?" She twirled around, as if showing off her clothes—men's sweatpants about three sizes too big, paired with a plaid flannel shirt that hung to her knees. She held up a plastic bag. "My real clothes are in here. They're a little wet."

Mia took one final sip from a glass of green juice and said, "Sit down and tell me everything."

"First, you tell me how you could drink that." Even Violet, lover of strange concoctions, shied away from green juice.

Mia shrugged. "It's kale! It's good for you. And before you leave this summer, I'll get you to drink it, too."

Violet giggled, highly doubting that would happen. Mia and Uncle Forrest's home could be a weird place, but that was one of the reasons she loved visiting.

Mia pulled out a seat for Violet, sat across the table, and looked at her expectantly. "I'm waiting," she reminded her cousin.

"Right." In a tumble of words, Violet told the whole story—about feeling awkward and upset around Hayes and not being able to do her job, and him picking up on her feelings and taking her to the shelter to cheer her up, right up to their almost-kiss.

Mia oohed and aahed and listened intently to every word. At the end, she hugged her cousin, happy for the turn of events. "But," she said, "you still have to face up to your fanfic."

She reached for her nearby laptop and opened it to the website, scrolling to the comments section. "I just checked this and read Lydia's message. You still haven't gotten back to her, have you?"

Violet shook her head.

Mia leaped to her feet, impatient for something to happen. "This could be your big break, and you're letting it slip through your fingers. How long do you think an agent as big as Lydia Jacobs is going to wait? She's probably reading through dozens of other fanfic stories right now, thinking you're a lost cause. She'll latch onto some other unknown writer and make him or her famous!"

"You don't know that."

"Of course I can't see the future. No one can. Although my dad insists his Ouija board can predict anything!" She shook her head to get back on topic. "The point is, you have to give yourself options . . . opportunities . . . not limits! You have to open the door to this. This is a once-in-a-lifetime chance and you don't want to regret turning it down before you even know what it is."

She squeezed Violet's hand. "Get in touch with Lydia. Set up a meeting. It's just two people talking, not a big deal at all. And once you get all the information, then you can make a decision."

Of course Mia was right. In her heart of hearts, Violet knew her cousin was just saying what Violet herself already thought. The only thing holding her back was the thought of hurting Hayes.

Mia turned the laptop toward Violet. "There. I've said my piece. Now get back to Lydia right now."

Quickly, Violet typed in that she could meet with Lydia first thing the next morning, if Lydia was free.

Almost immediately Lydia responded: *I can do eight.*

That would work, Violet typed. Their meeting was set. She grinned happily at Mia.

"Proud of you, cuz," Mia said. "Now just remember you have to tell Lydia your identity has to be kept secret. You have to be anonymous, until you talk to Hayes."

Violet didn't need any reminders about that. First Lydia, then Hayes. What could possibly go wrong?

The Imaginative International Talent Agency was in a modern office building on a wide, tree-lined block in Beverly Hills. Violet looked over a board in the lobby, listing companies and suites. She quickly found the agency; it took up four floors. Then she pressed the elevator button for the penthouse level, Lydia's office, and zipped up to the fortieth floor.

The door opened right into a lobby filled with tasteful

artwork, a few plush chairs, and a wide glass desk. The receptionist sitting behind it was as pretty as any model in a fashion magazine.

"May I help you?" the woman asked as Violet stepped into the room, her voice neutral.

"I'm Violet Reeves. I'm here to meet with Lydia Jacobs?" Violet's voice had risen in a question at the end of the sentence. She blushed, knowing she sounded like she was asking if she had an appointment, not stating a fact.

The woman looked at her blankly, and Violet realized Lydia didn't know her name. "I write the Hayes Grier fan fiction," she explained.

"Of course," the receptionist said smoothly. "She's expecting you. I'll take you to her office."

The woman rose from her chair with ballerina-like gracefulness. Violet followed her through a set of doors into an office that took up the rest of the floor. Windows reached from the rich white carpeting to the ceiling, revealing the LA skyline. It seemed more like a luxury apartment than an office, with living and dining areas, and not a file cabinet in sight.

"This is Violet Reeves," the receptionist announced, gliding smoothly out the door.

A small woman with straight dark hair, curved to her chin, walked around a mahogany table to greet her. Her first words: "How old are you?"

"I'm sixteen." Was there some kind of age requirement for writing fanfic?

"Aha!" Lydia said, delighted. "This gets better and better." She examined Violet closely. "Are you sure you're sixteen? Not seventeen, or eighteen?"

"Of course I'm sure."

"Well." Lydia waved at Violet to sit on a deep sectional couch in the corner. She paced in front of the couch in an exact square, shooting glances at Violet at every turn.

"This is impressive, then. You have such an authentic voice, my dear. Especially for one so young. Now tell me everything."

Violet explained about her World Famous Studios internship and her dream to get into the Hollywood Screenwriting Academy. She even mentioned the potential recommendation letter from director T. J. Meyers.

Lydia laughed merrily. "Recommendation letter? My dear, when I get through with you, you won't need any recommendation letter. The Academy will be begging you to attend!"

Violet's jaw dropped in surprise. She saw herself in the window's reflection and quickly closed her mouth. "What do you mean?"

"I'm ready to make you Hollywood's next big writer. Anyone who's anyone already wants to work with you. Everybody's been asking around, wanting to know who you are. And when they hear that you're only sixteen? They'll be beating down my door. If we play up the age angle, you'll be a huge unstoppable media sensation to boot."

Violet straightened her shoulders, holding herself back from jumping up and down like a six-year-old who just got a pony for her birthday. She was loving every word that came out of Lydia Jacobs's mouth.

Imagine! Little Violet Reeves from upstate New York, a nobody who thought she was incredibly lucky just to have a studio internship, could be making the rounds of talk shows. She'd be photographed because she was Violet, not someone's date. And she'd get to do what she always loved—write!

Violet pinched herself to make sure she wasn't dreaming—something she thought writers just made up. But no, she was doing it, and she wasn't dreaming. It was real.

"So what do you think, my dear?"

Violet came down to earth. She had to tell Lydia about her stipulation: She would only sign with the agency if Lydia agreed to keep her identity confidential.

"I have some personal business to take care of," Violet told her, "before I feel comfortable coming forward."

Finally, Lydia sat down. She thought for a moment, her chin in hand, her carefully made-up face tilted to the side.

"Agreed." She nodded twice. "But we can't wait too long. The reveal has to be soon. We have to strike while the iron is red-hot. You need to take care of this business quickly. And when I say quickly, I mean today."

They made an appointment to meet again, and Lydia walked Violet to the door. "My dear, I can't stress enough the importance of acting fast. An opportunity like this only comes around once. You need to jump on it."

"I understand, Lydia. I truly do."

"Good. And in the meantime, you should be asking yourself two questions." Lydia paused dramatically, making sure Violet was paying strict attention. "Why are you here if you're not ready to commit to this one hundred percent? And what is holding you back from fulfilling your dream?"

Violet had the rest of the morning off, so she went back home. The house was quiet. Uncle Forrest had gone to a yoga retreat, and Mia was taking an all-day art course at the college. Violet couldn't even text her the news; Mia was sketching live models, and Violet didn't want to distract her.

Humming tunelessly, she wandered through the house, not sure what to do next. She couldn't tell anyone else the news, not even her parents. Even worse, she didn't know exactly what to think.

At first she'd been euphoric, thrilled beyond belief that her writing career seemed set. But then there were Lydia's two questions . . .

Gnawing doubts hit her hard and suddenly. What *was* holding her back?

Violet knew the answer without giving it any thought: Hayes Grier.

Sighing, Violet went to her room, slipping off her shoes before she reached the bed. She stretched out, thinking about Hayes and what could happen between them. A first date. A first kiss. Something more . . .

She rolled on her side, half-closed her eyes, and pictured more scenarios. Then she sat up, her eyes snapping open. Is this how she was going to spend the morning?

At the desk, the computer seemed to beckon, the screen winking at her in the morning sunshine. Writing would help her decompress. She just needed to let go of reality for a bit. It would be a release, nothing more.

She turned on the computer, opening up her HollywoodWriter310 site. She placed her fingers on the keyboard and began . . .

> . . . *Hayes and Rose were having the summer of their lives. Each day was an adventure—hiking in Griffith Park, going to the movies, having bonfires at the beach—and they were growing closer and closer. Now Hayes had come to a decision. He wanted to take another step in their relationship. Show Rose a side of him she hadn't seen.*

"Saturday," he told her. "I have a surprise for you."

That morning, he blindfolded Rose and helped her into the front seat of his car. They drove through LA—Rose laughing all the way, trying to guess their destination, and Hayes refusing to give one little hint.

He pulled into a spot, helped her out, led her down the street, and stopped.

"Ready?"

"Ready," said Rose, breathlessly, with no idea what to expect.

Hayes removed the blindfold in one smooth move, and Rose gasped. They were standing in front of the Dog World Dog Shelter.

"Why are we here?" Rose stared at Hayes in surprise. Then, of course, it all made sense. Where else would Hayes Grier, animal lover, be?

"I volunteer here," Hayes said. "Tez is the only other person who knows about it. I haven't told anyone else; I really don't want it getting out. I share so much on social media, but not this. It means too much to me. And I don't want the place overrun! But I trust you. I want to share it with you."

Holding hands, the two walked inside.

They went straight into a playroom full of puppies chewing on toys, bounding after balls, and having fun. The puppies raced over to greet Hayes and Rose, barking happily. "I hope it can be 'our' place now, Rose. That we can be here together."

"Oh, Hayes." Rose leaned into him, and they kissed. One adorable puppy nuzzled their legs and Hayes scooped him up.

"I won't tell anyone," she promised, gazing at him over the puppy's head. "This will be our special secret . . ."

Violet read over the passage, picturing herself as Rose, because, well . . . she *was* clearly Rose! She smiled warmly, remembering every moment of the real visit. The writing worked; she felt calmer.

She loved the piece—reading it and writing it—but of course no one would ever see it. There were too many Hayes Grier personal details, and the animal-shelter setting revealed way too much.

She would never ever post it. It would be her own secret story to read when she was feeling down or confused.

Her phone alarm suddenly sounded, and Violet started. Thank goodness she'd set a reminder. Otherwise, she'd still be lounging around daydreaming.

But she had to get to the studio. Violet glanced at the time. *Now!* Hayes was shooting that final scene today; the tough emotional one, when he says good-bye to Devon. She had to be there to help him, to support him any way she could.

She cast one last wistful glance at the computer, then left for the lot. A moment later she raced back inside, taking the stairs two at a time. She'd forgotten to save the story!

She tapped the keyboard quickly, one eye on the clock, then left without a backward glance. She didn't see the screen a split second later when it flashed *Posting Complete*.

The shelter story had gone live.

CHAPTER SEVENTEEN

VIOLET STEPPED QUIETLY INTO THE TRAILER. She'd seen Hayes and Tez rehearsing through the window—Hayes pacing and Tez sitting on the couch reciting from the script. And she hadn't wanted to interrupt. Now she nodded at the two, signaling them to keep going.

Violet gazed around the space, missing the trailer, even though she was standing right inside it. Most likely her job would end today. The movie would wrap. And her time on set would be over. Zan rushed over to say hello, his tail wagging like crazy.

Violet crouched down to hug him close, listening to

Hayes say the lines "It's over, Devon. We're done. Go back home where you belong." His voice came out weak and strained.

"Shoot!" he cried in his normal tone. "That really stunk." Frustrated, he grunted and plopped on the couch, his head in his hands.

"Thank God you're here," he told Violet, lifting his head a second later. "It ain't workin' with Tez, that's for sure."

"Maybe because I'm not a sixteen-year-old girl with straight black hair." Tez grinned. "At least Violet's got the girl part down."

"And maybe Violet is a better acting coach, too," Hayes retorted, punching Tez in the arm. "Now get out of here."

"You want me to leave?" Tez feigned shock and despair. "But I need to be with you!"

"See?" Hayes pushed him toward the door. "You really can't act, bro."

As soon as the door closed behind Tez, Hayes reached for Violet's hand, gently drawing her to the couch. "Can we take it from the top?"

"Sure," Violet agreed. "Let's run through the entire scene."

They went through the beginning lines, Hayes nailing each one like a pro. But when it came to the lines she'd heard him rehearse with Tez, starting with "It's over, Devon. We're done," Hayes lost focus. He spoke in a dull voice, and Violet knew he was looking ahead to the next bit—dreading it, really—when his eyes were supposed to cloud with anguish and one lone tear trickle down his cheek.

"It wasn't Tez!" Hayes paced the floor, frustration turning his face red. "It's me! It's me, V. I can't connect to the scene. I just can't act!"

"Hayes, shush." Violet strode closer to settle him down. "It will be okay. Come sit."

They moved to the couch, and Violet thought for a minute. "Okay, I have some ideas that could help."

Hayes brightened. "I'll try anything."

"Let's concentrate on the emotion. All we have to do is come up with a scenario that would bring out those same feelings you need here."

Hayes nodded, listening closely.

"Think about how you'd feel if you had to protect Zan, and the best way for you to do that was to give him up. Then substitute Zan for Devon."

They went through the lines, but right in the middle, Hayes snorted with laughter. "Sorry, V. I'm literally putting Zan in Devon's place. I keep picturing him wearing Devon's shorts and tank top. I think I'm getting punchy."

"Okay, let's stick with Devon, the girl." Violet considered a new angle. "Try getting really angry at the bad guys. Think what you had to give up to fight them! Then try and turn that anger into sadness."

That run-through was a little better, but Hayes still seemed to flounder at the end.

"Any other ideas?" he asked tiredly.

"How about this. You've just given up everything you love. Imagine how determined you'd be to save the world. That's all you have left."

"Loss transformed into determination. I like it."

Hayes rose and recited the lines again. Something was still off.

"Let's face it. Nothing is working. This final scene is the most important part of the movie. The success of the entire film hinges on these lines. If I can't get it right, I'll be the reason *The Midnight Hawk* fails. And you know what? I just can't do it."

"Yes, you can," Violet insisted. She couldn't let him give up. She looked at Hayes sitting next to her, slumped against the couch, his eyes closed in exhaustion. He had to make this happen. Acting was so important to him—as important as her writing was to her.

If she were writing this scene, how would she get the creative juices flowing? Of course, she didn't really have an answer. She'd tried to write a new screenplay and had been hit by writer's block right between the eyes. Still, she'd kept writing. She'd just turned to fanfic. Why did that come so much easier?

Violet sat up straight, the answer suddenly crystal clear. Because she wasn't trying so hard!

"I have one more idea," she told Hayes. "Take a deep breath and close your eyes. Clear your mind."

Hayes nodded, breathing in deeply and shutting his eyes.

"Now open your eyes, put the script facedown, and say your lines without trying to act. Just say them," she repeated, "and see what happens."

Hayes turned over the pages. He stood, opening his mouth to begin, when Derek stuck his head inside the trailer.

"You're needed on set right now," he told Hayes.

Hayes nodded calmly, but as soon as Derek closed the door, he looked at Violet in a panic.

"Just go." She ushered him out, smiling gently. "I believe in you. I believe in your talent. I know you have this in you, Hayes. Now, go show everybody else."

Hayes stood at the edge of the lot, trying to pull himself together. He squinted up at the hill, the spot where he'd say his good-bye to Devon, wishing he had just a little more time. If only he could walk away and come back tomorrow, surely he'd have the emotion down by then. Even a few more minutes would help. Maybe, if he ducked out right now, no one would notice.

He began to edge away . . .

"Hayes!" TJ rushed over. "You're here! We're all ready for you. Just remember, you and Devon have already been through so much together. You know what you have to do, but it's so hard. You love her. She's stuck by you . . ."

TJ went on for a bit longer, pointing out marks Hayes had to hit so the camera would track him and interrupting himself to shout instructions to the crew.

Hayes followed TJ from spot to spot, his eyes open wide like a deer caught in headlights. "Steady, guy," he whispered to himself. "You got this. Just listen to Violet. Just clear your head, then say the words without trying to act. Just be. Just be Hawk."

"I am Hawk!" he said out loud, like suddenly everything had clicked.

Violet, just sneaking onto the set, heard him and grinned.

"Of course you're Hawk," TJ said exasperatedly. "You've been playing him for days now!"

Standing in the shadows, Violet smothered a laugh. Sometimes, TJ could be so clueless. She watched Hayes and Coco take their marks, standing close together under the setting sun.

Violet concentrated on Hayes's face, not the words they exchanged. At first his expression was hard, almost cruel, as he told Devon their relationship was over. She was on her own. Then, as soon as she turned to leave, his face changed. His features shifted and softened, his eyes clouded with pain. Violet felt a pull on her heart; his sadness was overwhelming.

One lone tear slid down his cheek. A muscle twitched in his jaw. But Hayes was still, not wiping the tear, not moving. Not doing anything but being Hawk.

"Cut!" TJ shouted. "That's it! We got it. One take! That's all you needed, Hayes. You nailed it!"

Violet stepped into the open, smiling and laughing, feeling as though Hayes's success was her own.

"V!" Hayes spied her and raced over, ignoring everyone trying to congratulate him. He lifted her in the air and spun her around until she was dizzy. "Did you see that? One take! All because of you!"

Hayes set her gently on the ground and smiled at her. "Thank you so much for all your help. I couldn't have gotten here without you, without someone I trust helping me."

Violet blinked and tried to keep smiling. But the word *trust* brought her back to reality with a thud. She still had to talk to Hayes. She still had to tell him about the fanfic.

But Hayes was so happy now. And she was so happy for him. She couldn't take the focus away from his success, not when he'd struggled so hard and had done so well.

Was she just making excuses? Just postponing the inevitable?

Let's face it, she thought. *I'm totally dreading his reaction.*

She gazed at his face beaming with joy. Her heart skipped a beat. She had to do it. Right now.

"So, thank you, thank you!" Hayes repeated, hugging her tightly.

"Excuse me, guys, best friend coming through." Tez tapped Hayes on the shoulder, and Hayes broke the embrace to give him a high five. "Bro, you rocked!" Tez said. "And you rock, too, Violet. Whatever you told him in the trailer worked like crazy."

"He was great!" Violet agreed.

"Listen, I need to talk to you, dude," Tez said to Hayes.

"That's okay." Violet stepped away to give them space. Maybe Tez wanted to talk about Mia. Maybe not. Either way, she should get her own thoughts together and figure out the best way to talk to him. She'd do it as soon as Tez left.

"Have you seen this?" Tez was saying, holding out his phone for Hayes to see.

Violet couldn't help but listen in. The two were so cute together.

"What?" said Hayes.

"It's that Hayes Grier fanfic. You know those stories about you that are so popular?" Tez sounded anxious and angry.

Violet groaned. Why was Tez so on edge? He'd already seen all her entries, including the last one set at the prom.

"I haven't had a chance to read it! You think I have any time outside this movie?"

"The author wrote about you volunteering at the dog

shelter. I thought that was under wraps. Weren't you keeping that private on purpose? I mean, who is writing this stuff?"

Hayes grabbed Tez's phone. He scanned the site, scrolling down the length of the screen. His face turned pale. He opened his mouth to speak, but no words came out. He'd been shocked speechless.

As she listened, Violet's face drained of color, too. She stumbled, feeling faint. How could this have happened? The animal shelter story online? It wasn't possible! She thought back to earlier in the day . . . running back to the room to save the story . . . hitting a key without looking, too worried about the time to pay attention.

A knot formed in the pit of her stomach and she leaned against a wall. She must have hit the wrong key. She didn't just save the story as a draft. She posted it!

Somehow, Violet got through the afternoon, avoiding Hayes and anyone else who tried to say more than hello. The filming was done. Everyone had been excited and happy, and no one noticed Violet sneak away early—except, of course, TJ.

"Leaving so soon?" he'd asked.

"I—I'm not really feeling well," Violet had answered. It was true. She felt sick to her stomach.

TJ looked closely at her face and nodded. "You look awful. Go home and get some rest before the wrap party. You know it's tomorrow night, right?"

Violet had nodded, escaping into her car. And now, at home, she felt relieved, ready to collapse on her bed and figure out what to do.

She opened the front door to a darkened living room. A single candle stood on the floor. Uncle Forrest sat in a meditative pose before it, holding a clear quartz crystal tied to a string. He swung the crystal like a pendulum, slowly, over the flame. "Oh, rays of light. Oh, stars and sun. Oh, blessings of harmony—Oh, Violet!"

Uncle Forest rose to his feet to embrace his niece. "You're home!"

"What's going on, Uncle Forrest?"

"I'm performing a crystal healing ritual. I've been sensing a dark aura around this house. There are feelings of pain . . . feelings of guilt . . . a darkness is falling that needs to be lit." He paused. "Have you eaten dinner? There's pesto pizza in the fridge."

"I'm not hungry."

Uncle Forrest brought the candle closer to Violet's face. He peered anxiously into her eyes. "Perhaps the darkness is coming from you, Violet. You seem upset. I can help. I can help heal you with crystal therapy." He paused. "Or perhaps a simple aura cleanse?"

His eyes were kind, full of concern, and Violet nestled closer to him. "That's okay, Uncle Forrest. I wish it were that simple. Unless you have a crystal that can turn back time?"

Wouldn't that be amazing? she thought. To get a do-over, to start at the very beginning with Hayes and tell him about the fanfic right away.

"Sadly, no." He laughed gently. "But at least I can do this." He reached for her photo above the fireplace, a picture from her elementary school graduation. Then he moved it to a table, placing the candle next to it. He dipped the crystal in a bowl of water and held it up so water drops fell, and the candlelight refracted into rainbow beams.

"Pain and guilt transform to joy," he intoned, swinging the crystal over the picture. "And Violet?"

"Yes, Uncle Forrest?"

"Mia is upstairs if you want to talk."

Violet trudged upstairs, debating whether to tell Mia what happened. Would it make her feel better or worse?

"Violet!" Mia poked her head out of the bedroom, and the decision was taken out of her hands. Mia pulled Violet inside, closing the door, then turned to her excitedly. "I'm so glad you're here!" She pointed to her laptop screen. "I've just read your latest installment. It's awesome. It seems so real, like you're standing right there with Hayes in the dog shelter."

Violet sighed, throwing herself on Mia's bed and squeezing her eyes shut to block out the world.

"What's wrong? It's a great story. It's so much more rich and deep somehow, more rooted and real between the characters. And now that Hayes knows the truth, it's all good, right?"

"Hayes doesn't know!" Violet almost wailed.

"You haven't told him?"

Violet shook her head. "And I really did go to an animal shelter with Hayes, and something almost like this happened. But we never kissed! And this piece is way too revealing. Too personal. Hayes doesn't want this information out there. It was all a secret, until I posted it—by accident!"

Mia's eyes opened wide. "So now what?"

"Now it needs to come down." It was the only answer. Maybe she could stop a few people, at least, from reading it. "In fact," she went on, "I want all of it to go away."

"You mean take down every story?"

"Yes, all of it," she repeated. "Can you help me?"

The girls pulled up chairs to the desk and worked furiously. A few minutes later, the screen was blank. The stories were gone. Violet felt a pang. Her best work had just disappeared without a trace. But it was for the best.

Violet leaned back in the chair, trying to give herself a pep talk.

She'd told herself this many times: She had to go to Hayes

and tell him the truth. And now there were no excuses. Hayes had finished filming. He wasn't disappointed about the motorcycle stunt or stressed about his big scene. It was over. And everyone knew he was terrific.

Violet couldn't blame bad timing, not anymore.

Violet's internship was done, too, and she had no script to show TJ. If he refused to read anything of hers again . . . well, so be it. She was okay with it. And if Hayes refused to ever talk to her again? Well, she was not okay with that, but she'd understand. She deserved it.

Tomorrow night was the wrap party. She'd do it there. She'd tell Hayes the truth, the whole truth—her feelings and her mistakes.

It was her moment to finally be honest. She was almost looking forward to it.

Violet slept late the next morning, then lounged around the house, trying to relax. She flipped through channels on TV. She cleaned her room. She even started a screenplay about a high school student who comes to Hollywood on a summer internship and totally messes up. She figured, write what you know. And she certainly knew about that.

Once she started, the writing actually went pretty well. Just as it happened with the fanfic, Violet lost track of time. When she finally turned away from the computer screen, she jumped to her feet. She had to start getting ready! And she hadn't given a thought to what she should wear. She lifted a lock of hair and let it fall limply to her shoulders. Did she still have time to shampoo?

Wind chimes sounded at the front door. Violet paused, hoping someone would answer it. But apparently, nobody else was home. The chimes rang again.

Hurriedly, Violet made her way downstairs, then peered through the small window on the door. Two bright hazel eyes looked back, framed by sleek black hair.

Coco? Violet drew in her breath. What was she doing here, when the wrap party was starting in an hour? She swung open the door and gasped. Coco wasn't alone.

"Hey, girl." Coco stepped inside, not waiting for an invitation. "I'm here with my glam squad."

"I see that!" An entourage of stylists marched in behind Coco, all smiling, all holding trays of blush, mascara, hair gel, straightening irons, and more. Two women from wardrobe pulled clothing racks filled with dresses and gowns.

Everyone paused in the hall. "Where should we set up?" Coco asked brightly.

A few minutes later, Violet's room looked like a combination beauty salon, spa, and upscale boutique.

"Why did you do all this?" Violet asked Coco as they settled into chairs, stylists spraying their hair.

"Isn't it obvious?" Coco joked. "So we can get ready for the party!"

"No, I mean really." Violet gazed at the racks of clothes, each one more glamorous than the last.

Coco smiled at her. "Seriously, you're the first real friend I've made in ages who isn't all 'Hollywood.' This is my way of thanking you. Besides, we never had that girls' night out, right? So this is our time! Let's enjoy it!"

An hour later, the girls walked out of the house, heads held high. Violet wore a sequined red dress with spaghetti straps and red high heels. Coco was dressed almost identically but in white.

Violet caught sight of herself in the mirror on the way out and nodded at her reflection.

"Yup," said Coco happily. "We look like a million bucks."

Violet had to laugh. After tonight . . . after explaining everything to Hayes . . . their relationship might very well be over. Her life would be in pieces. But at least she'd look her best!

CHAPTER EIGHTEEN

COCO'S DRIVER TOOK them to a Hollywood Hills mansion overlooking the twinkling lights of LA. Photographers snapped pictures of Coco—and Violet—on the way in. But the paparazzi stayed outside.

Violet was glad no cameras could capture her dumbstruck expression when she stepped through the doors. *Mansion* was an understatement. The girls walked through the marble entrance hall into a huge open space. "The grand salon," Coco whispered to her.

Chandeliers hung from the ceiling. Two grand pianos stood next to each other in a corner. The polished wooden floors gleamed. A band, its members dressed in tuxedos, played jazz on a raised platform. The waitstaff circled, offering crab cakes, sushi, and minifoods Violet didn't recognize.

In fact, she barely recognized the partygoers filling the room. On set, everyone had dressed casually. Here, they looked as if they'd stepped out of a fashion magazine.

It was all glitz, all glamour, and it took her breath away.

But where was Hayes? She peered around the room. Finally she spied him, way on the other side, wearing a sharp gray blazer and a baseball cap, talking to Tez.

Now, she told herself. *Talk to him now.*

Violet took a deep breath, excused herself, and made her way across the crowded room. She was almost there when TJ stepped in front of her.

"Violet!" he exclaimed, like she was just the person he wanted to see.

"TJ!" she responded, craning her neck to look around him, trying to catch sight of Hayes.

"I'm trying to talk to as many people as I can tonight," TJ was saying. "I know I can be a little difficult at times, and I'd like, in my own way, to make amends."

Violet raised her eyebrows but held back from saying, "A little?"

TJ plowed on. "But you did a lot for this movie, Violet. You really took care of Hayes. You did an exceptional job, and I hope we can work together again."

Pleased, Violet said, "Thanks, TJ."

"And," he added, "I can't wait to read your new script."

"I'm still working on it," she told TJ, not mentioning she'd just started it earlier that day. "You'll have it soon."

Maybe now, with her days free—no movie, no fanfic— she could really get cracking.

By now TJ was gazing over her shoulder, scouting out the next person to talk to, and Violet slipped away. She hurried to the spot she'd seen Hayes, but now he and Tez were gone.

Her eyes swept the room, lighting on Tez getting a drink—no Hayes in sight—then on a crew of production assistants goofing around, balancing spoons on their noses. And there was Coco, standing behind a potted plant, flirting with another PA. Violet smiled. That must be the mystery man. The guy Coco wanted to make jealous. He was cute! And he seemed into Coco. Violet felt glad for her friend. Coco may be a teenage star, but she really did like to stay away from Hollywood celebs.

Then Violet glimpsed a baseball cap moving through the crowd. Hayes. *It's now or never*, she told herself. For a moment she closed her eyes, focusing on her speech. *Hayes, here I come.* She stepped forward.

But once again, someone was stopping her, tapping her shoulder from behind. She turned around, annoyed. Then she smiled. "Hayes!"

"Hey, V. You're a hard girl to find. I've been searching the whole party for you."

Violet felt a tingle—he'd been looking for her!—quickly followed by a wave of nausea. This was it.

"Come with me," Hayes said, taking her hand. "There's something I want to show you."

Violet trembled—from nerves or excitement, she couldn't tell. She held on as Hayes led her through the room. Something was going to happen. She just didn't know what.

Hayes took Violet outside, through a rose garden lined by tall hedges, to a dimly lit path. They walked a bit more, seeing fewer and fewer people, until they stopped in a grassy circle. They were alone. The sounds of the party drifted over on a warm breeze, but Violet felt like she and Hayes were a million miles away.

"What is it?" she asked, a little breathlessly. They were face-to-face. In heels, she was almost his height. "What did you want me to see?"

"Look up," he whispered, his breath tickling her ear. As she lifted her eyes, Hayes said, "Stars! There's no smog tonight. I bet we can see them all."

It was true. Hundreds upon hundreds of stars glowed brightly in the clear night sky. "I thought you'd like the view."

Now she lowered her gaze, staring directly into his eyes. "I do like the view," she said. Hayes wrapped her in his arms. Violet's heart thumped wildly. But she had to get herself together. She had to tell him the truth. She stepped away.

"Thank you, Hayes," she said, "for bringing me out here." She felt herself move closer to him again, as if pulled by a magnet. "I'm glad we're alone. There's something I need to tell you."

"V, let me go first. I have something to say, too." He grinned at her, his eyes snapping with excitement, like a little kid with a big secret he can't wait to share. "Please?"

Violet couldn't say no; she nodded.

Now Hayes drew back so he could look her full in the face. "I like you, V. I mean I really like you, as a lot more than a friend. And I think you may like me, too. I can trust you, V. And I've never felt this way with a girl before."

Violet drew in her breath. *Trust*. Once she said her piece, he'd never feel that way again. The trust would be shattered. She opened her mouth to speak, but before she could say a word, Hayes's lips met hers. He threaded his hands through her hair and kissed her slowly, oh so slowly, and so tenderly, she felt her insides melt. The kiss was sweet and soft; so perfect, Violet couldn't have written it better in her fanfic.

Finally, they broke apart, both with a sort of a gasp, both smiling so widely, Violet felt her cheeks stretch. They stared at each other, speechless.

"So, Violet!" A loud voice interrupted the moment. "This is where all those fanfic ideas come from."

Violet turned, trying to move from one minute to the next, from sweet rapture to harsh reality. The words didn't register. "What?" she said.

TJ loomed in front of her, hands on his hips. "The Hayes Grier fanfic. All those romantic stories. They're yours. You're the mystery writer."

Violet's stomach dropped. She didn't know what to do— deny it all, confess in front of everyone, or run away. How did he even find out?

Lydia stepped out from behind TJ's shadow. *That's how*, Violet quickly realized. The talent agent had told him, revealing Violet's secret before she could explain it to Hayes, her way.

"Hayes . . ." Violet turned to him, her eyes welling. He'd moved away from her, his eyes wide open in disbelief, darting from TJ to Lydia to Violet.

"Let me explain."

"So it's true," he said slowly, as if every word was an effort to get out. "You wrote about the dog shelter and all the stuff I wanted to keep quiet."

"I didn't mean—" Violet began.

"You betrayed my trust," he said, the words coming out fast and strong now. "You lied to me." Then, before she could say another word, he turned, disappearing into the darkness.

"Hayes, wait!" Violet lurched forward. But TJ held her arm, keeping her back.

"You don't have to show me that second script," he was saying, grinning wildly. "Don't bother. I want to work with you on this fanfic project. No doubt about it. And the rec? Consider it done!"

Violet felt like screaming. Work was the last thing on her mind. "Thank you. But I've got to go!"

She raced after Hayes, tripping over roots, stumbling over stones. She found him at the end of the path, sitting against a tree.

"Hayes." Violet leaned over to catch her breath, then sat beside him. "I'm so sorry. I was just about to tell you, you must know that. I just feel so—"

"Forget it, Violet." Hayes's voice was harsh. "Save your breath. I thought I could trust you. I thought you understood me better than anyone I'd met in my entire life. I opened up to you. And you exploited it . . . you exploited *me* . . . just to get ahead." He stood, looking down at her angrily. "I never want to see you again."

"Hayes," she begged.

But he was already gone.

PART THREE

Girl Loses Boy

CHAPTER NINETEEN

A SUDDEN BURST of sunshine lit the bedroom. Violet pulled the covers over her head. "Close the curtains, Mia!"

"No," said Mia, opening them even wider. "It's one o'clock! I've already eaten breakfast and lunch, and you haven't even gotten out of bed." She moved closer to the bed and flung off the blanket.

"I'm wallowing!" Violet sniffled. "Can't you leave me in peace?"

"You've been wallowing for three weeks now." Mia's voice softened. "I know it's been hard. Did you check your phone today? Maybe Hayes sent something this morning."

"I doubt it." Still, Violet struggled to sit up, reaching for her phone on the nightstand. She checked for messages. "No, nothing. I've sent Hayes dozens of texts. Maybe hundreds! It's been so long now, and he hasn't gotten back to me at all."

"I still can't believe Lydia told TJ that you wrote the fanfic. She promised she wouldn't say anything until you said it was okay!"

Violet sighed. "I can't really blame her. TJ said he wanted to collaborate with the fanfic author for his next project. Lydia couldn't help herself. She thought she was looking out for a client.

"If TJ had stormed over a few minutes later, everything could have been different. I would have already told Hayes. But this whole mess is totally my fault."

Mia moved next to Violet, settling against the headboard. "Well, I'll let you stay in bed a little longer, then we're getting out of the house. You're only here another week. You have to make the most of it. So stop thinking about Hayes! Think about something else!" She picked up the remote. "Let's see what's on."

She flicked on the TV. On-screen, a sitcom family was eating breakfast, the kids arguing with their parents about cleaning their rooms. Mia switched channels to car racing. She pressed the remote again. A cooking show. She pressed again. The *Hollywood This Week* logo appeared, followed by the show's anchor, Rick Rodgerson, announcing an exclusive on Hayes Grier, coming up next.

Violet reached for the remote and made it louder. The scene cut to Alison Portnoy, standing in front of a framed *Midnight Hawk* movie poster. Violet remembered looking over all the photos with Hayes, trying to choose one. It came down to two: a solo shot with Hayes, his sweatshirt hood pulled up, half-covering his face, running along a dark street, looking anxiously over his shoulder.

The other was a close-up, a shot of his grimy face, a determined glint in his eye, ready to take on the bad guys. Remembering how close they'd been, how they both pointed to the running shot at the very same time, felt like a knife through her heart.

"You're hearing it here first," Alison Portnoy was saying. "Sixteen-year-old sensation Hayes Grier is gearing up for a world tour following the premiere of his new movie. He is the Midnight Hawk, a starring role that's already generating Oscar buzz. The premiere is scheduled in two days, and Hayes will be catching a private jet the very next morning to meet his fans across the globe. Go to our website and check his tour schedule; he may be coming to your town soon!"

"He's leaving?" Violet switched off the TV, burrowing under the blankets once more. She hiccuped in despair.

Mia patted her awkwardly. "I love you, Mia, but can you leave me alone for a bit?" A sob escaped. "I need to be by myself."

"Oh, Violet!" Mia waited a moment, clearly hoping Violet would change her mind. Finally, she stood uncertainly, hovering over the bed. "You'll call me if you need anything?"

Under the covers, Violet nodded.

"Okay, well, I'll be in my room all afternoon. Forget leaving the house. I'm not going anywhere, at least until I feel better about you."

Mia left, closing the door softly behind her. As soon as she was gone, Violet cried harder. *Now what?* she wondered. *What can I possibly do?*

Keep busy, she told herself. Hayes wasn't the only one leaving. She'd be getting on an airplane soon, too, heading back home.

Sighing, Violet gazed around the messy room. She'd barely picked up after herself since the wrap party. It looked as bad as Hawk's bedroom set, with piled-up bowls and dirty clothes. She had to get her stuff together. Like it or not, she had to get moving.

Violet organized her clothes into groups: dirty, somewhat dirty, and clean enough to pack as is. She pulled a sweatshirt from under the bed and saw something stuck under its sleeve: the photo-booth pictures from Hayes's party.

She sat down heavily, looking at the two of them—grinning, goofy, serious. Looking as if they were ready to fall in love. And she burst into tears once more.

Okay, that was it. She had to get out. Slipping into a pair of sweats and not bothering to look in the mirror or change her pajama top, she snuck past Mia's room and out the back door.

The boardwalk by Venice Beach was crowded with tourists. Violet felt invisible, glad she could fade into the sea of people. No one here knew—or cared—that she'd just betrayed the guy of her dreams.

The fresh air felt good; the ocean glistened in the distance. Violet took deep, long breaths, hoping to breathe in the good, breathe out the bad.

If only Uncle Forrest could hear me now! she thought, managing a smile. *He'd be so proud.*

An hour later, Violet was turning to go home, a little more ready to tackle her room, when Jay fell into step beside her.

"Hey, stranger," he said, smiling, a beach towel slung over his shoulder.

"Jay!"

Violet had spoken to him after the beach party, explaining she was already semi-involved with somebody else, and apologizing for kissing him. The timing wasn't right for them to start anything. He'd nodded, saying, "Okay, fine," in a curt kind of way, and that was all. She hadn't seen him since.

But now Jay was smiling, seemingly glad to see her.

"How are you?" she asked.

Jay gave her a friendly nudge. "I guess I can't complain." He looked at her sideways. "Not everything this summer worked out the way I wanted. But I aced those classes and I'm feeling pretty good now. You, on the other hand, don't look too happy."

He added more seriously, "Is everything okay?"

Violet sighed. She looked at Jay; his hair had lightened, his tan had deepened. He looked in shape and seriously cute. If only she had fallen for him instead of Hayes, this walk home would be so different. They'd be laughing and holding hands, knowing they had precious little time left together and enjoying every second.

Instead, she was on her own, miserable and angry about every wrong decision she'd made. For a moment she wished she'd never met Hayes, never gotten the internship. But she knew she didn't mean it. Just knowing him had been worth it.

And Jay? He was a great guy. She hadn't given him enough credit before; he'd been nothing but kind.

"Things could be better," Violet admitted.

"Want to talk about it?"

Violet shook her head. "I don't really want to get into it. But thanks for being a friend."

Jay blushed a bit under his tan. "I'm glad I got to know you. I'm sorry if this summer wasn't everything you wanted it to be, either."

Violet closed her eyes. She was sorry, too.

A few minutes later, Violet said good-bye to Jay and paused on her front steps. She picked up a package resting by the door, about the size of a pillow, and almost as light. She squeezed it. Whatever was inside was soft. "Mia," she called, walking inside. "Something came for you."

"Violet?" Mia rushed downstairs, looking surprised. She gazed at Violet, wearing sweats, sneakers, and a pajama top. "You went out?"

"I needed air."

"Did it help?"

"Not really." She held out the package for Mia. "There's no return address."

"Let's go into the kitchen," Mia said, already ripping it open. "Hey, look at this!" She let the contents fall onto the kitchen table: three T-shirts, all Hayes Grier merchandise, with the graphics Mia had designed. Each one was a combination photo and black-line drawing.

On the front of the first, Hayes sat on a sketch-drawing of a motorcycle, staring straight ahead, coming at you. The back had Hayes on the same motorcycle, leaving. On the front of the second, Hayes and Zan sat on a black-line drawing of a couch, looking forward; the back of the couch and the backs of their heads were pictured on the other side. The third T-shirt featured Hayes taking a selfie with a line-drawn phone. On the front he faced forward. The other side showed his back, but his face in the phone.

The words were the same on all three: *Coming* . . . *going* . . . *living*.

"Oh my God, these are amazing!" Mia skipped around the room. "I can't believe they came out so well!" She slowed to a walk, then stopped in front of Violet.

"I shouldn't be so happy when you feel so sad," she said, hugging her cousin briefly.

"But I'm happy for you." Violet hugged Mia back. "They look awesome."

"Don't give up!" Mia said suddenly, sounding fierce.

"What?"

"You're leaving soon, Violet, and so is Hayes. You don't have any time left! You can't just wait around doing nothing. Try texting Hayes one last time to apologize. Please! It couldn't make you feel any worse!"

That was true. At this point, Violet really had nothing to lose. "Okay," she agreed. "One last time."

She went to her room, sat on her bed, thought a moment, and then typed: *I know you leave for your tour in two days, but I wanted to try one last time to say I'm sorry. I feel horrible about what I did. I'd really like to see you so I can apologize in person. I hope you'll consider it. If not, I won't bother you again. Violet*

Violet sat holding her phone for fifteen long minutes. She didn't move; she barely breathed. She didn't dare look away from the screen for fear of missing Hayes's answer.

There wasn't one.

Violet couldn't sit there forever; finally she got up, taking the phone with her. When she showered, she put it on the ledge with the shampoo. When she made pasta for lunch, she kept it on the cutting board, right next to the chopped kale she was using for salad. She'd refused kale juice every time Uncle Forrest and Mia offered it—she had her limits, she'd joked. But she actually liked kale with apples and almonds.

After lunch, she slipped the phone in her jeans pocket and carried it with her everywhere.

Hayes never replied.

Then it was nighttime. At ten o'clock, Violet gave up. She turned off the phone, putting it facedown on her nightstand, just in case it miraculously turned back on.

She needed to face facts. She'd never see Hayes again, except on-screen or on a T-shirt.

———

"What are you doing here?"

Violet was sitting in TJ's office the next afternoon, trying not to think of all those other times she'd sat there, going over Hayes's schedule, taking notes on wardrobe and script changes, bringing coffee. Those days of caffeinated activity were over. No more running around trying to do ten things at once, with thoughts of Hayes Grier coloring every errand with a romantic glow.

Now TJ was sticking his head into the office, sounding annoyed she was there at all.

"We do have a meeting," Violet said tersely.

TJ strode inside, walking around the desk to ruffle Violet's hair. "Just playing with you," he said, smiling. "Of course we have a meeting!"

He sat down across from her, reached into the top desk drawer, and pulled out an envelope. "Here's the recommendation letter."

"What?"

"I wrote you a letter. I told you I'd write one for you, with or without another script." He eyed her empty hands. "And I guess it's without."

"I did have one idea, and it started out really well. But then I got stuck." Violet didn't bother to say she was stuck in bed, wallowing in misery about how things turned out with Hayes. She hadn't been able to write one more word, let alone an entire screenplay.

"I can show you nine pages."

"Not necessary." TJ paused. "But tell you what. Send it to me when it's done—whenever you finish it—and I'd be really happy to read it. In the meantime, you're pretty much a shoo-in for the Hollywood Screenwriting Academy now."

Violet looked at him, and her eyes filled with tears. He was being so nice . . . so un-TJ-like! But maybe she was being unfair. He had taught her a lot after all, and not just about cappuccino. "I feel horrible," she blurted, "about the way I hurt Hayes."

"I know." TJ looked back, a sympathetic expression on his face. "Don't tell anyone this, I don't want to damage my reputation for being a joker, but I've been thinking about what happened. And I think, deep down, you already know what to do."

From another drawer, he pulled out a paper copy of the Hayes Grier fanfic. "I printed out the stories," he said apologetically. "That's how good I think they are." Then he ripped them into shreds. "But they need a revision."

Slowly, Violet nodded. She got it. She had to rewrite the story and, this time, tell the truth.

It would be her apology piece. Her final one.

Violet stood. She had two days before Hayes began his

tour around the world, and one day before the *Midnight Hawk* premiere. Could she finish before then?

She had to give the new story as much heart as she gave the original fanfic.

And she had to do it fast.

CHAPTER TWENTY

ALL THAT DAY, Violet composed scenes and dialogue in her head, rejecting them one by one. Too sappy. Too boring. Just not right. But in the morning, she woke refreshed, with a perfect setting in her mind's eye. The beach.

In her room, Violet scribbled a DO NOT DISTURB sign and taped it outside her door. Then she sat at the desk, wearing sweats and slippers, a glass of water beside her. She glanced once at the clock, turned on the laptop, and typed furiously . . .

Violet and Hayes were sitting next to each other on Venice Beach. They shared a blanket but sat as far apart as possible. Violet stared straight ahead at the setting sun casting its colors across the sky. She was afraid to turn, to get so much as a glimpse of Hayes's face. She felt amazed and grateful he had even agreed to meet her. Looking at him—with such longing and emotion—could send him running. And she wouldn't blame him if he did run—fast and far away.

Hayes had opened up to her, and though she didn't mean to—not at all!—she'd basically slammed a door right in his face.

But this was her only chance; her opportunity to explain and apologize for what she'd done.

"Fan fiction is fiction," Violet began tentatively. "Rose is a character. But I wanted her to be me . . ."

"Rose. Violet. Flowers. I get it." Hayes spoke in monosyllables. But at least he was talking. Violet took heart.

"I'm just a regular girl. I didn't grow up in LA, I grew up clear across the country. And like anyone else, I watched movies on-screen. I sat, transfixed, watching stories unfold. I dreamed of becoming a screenwriter. I came

here to live those dreams. But something unexpected happened. I became an assistant— an assistant for a cute celebrity—and started to have feelings for the guy.

"Meanwhile, I tried to write a script, to make my dream come true. But I froze; I couldn't do it. For the first time ever, words didn't come. Maybe because the guy was the only thing I could think about. And when I finally started to write, he was all I could write about. Now the words—the fan fiction—were coming fast and furiously. Like a volcano erupting, I couldn't hold them back. It was a story just for me. 'No one else will ever see it,' I told myself. But then a friend saw it on-screen. She posted it without my knowledge or permission."

Finally Hayes turned to look at her, surprised.

"And the story took off. People around the country read it. Readers begged for more. And I had to write more. It became a need, a way to understand my feelings, to deal with everything I felt. I was so confused and in too deep, and the words kept coming."

Violet touched his arm. "I planned to tell you the truth. Remember when I pulled back *from the kiss by the Hollywood Sign? That was because I hadn't told you yet. But then Tez called with the emergency at your house. Over and over, I tried, but something would always happen—someone interrupted, or you had a big scene to deal with. It was never the right time. And yes, I took the easy way out, putting off what I should have done as soon as the fanfic went live. But I couldn't bear to upset you, or put a wedge between us. Not when our relationship was just beginning.*

"I never meant to betray you or use you. I'm so, so sorry. I can't even begin to tell you how sorry. One day, I hope you can find a way to trust me again. And if you can't, at least maybe you can forgive me."

Violet took a deep breath. "Hayes, what do you say?"

Violet couldn't finish the story. She didn't know the ending.

"Mia!" Violet called her cousin in to read the piece. She watched her, chewing her thumbnail anxiously. "Well?" she said when Mia spun around in the desk chair to face her.

Mia had tears in her eyes. "You outdid yourself, Violet. I am totally blown away. It's so . . . so heartfelt. I guess the truth always is. It's going to rock the fanfic world."

"There's only one reader I care about."

"I know." Mia touched her hand. "Are you going to post it?"

Violet nodded. Her hand trembling just slightly, she hit the POST button, then closed her eyes. More than anything in the world, she wanted this to work. She only had one more thing to do. She picked up her phone to send a text.

Coco's phone buzzed. "'Scuse me a sec," she told Hayes, checking the text.

They were sitting in a booth at the Coffee Break, sharing a chocolate chip scone, not really talking, just keeping each other company. Coco was treating Hayes—a thank-you for helping to get Barry, that cute production assistant, to notice her. But he wasn't asking questions about the relationship, and Coco didn't want to rub his nose in a happy romance. Clearly, Hayes wasn't interested in talking about anything that had happened between him and Violet, either. So Coco, uncharacteristically, was silent.

Coco sighed, stirring her caramel coffee shake that didn't need mixing. She'd just seen Violet's text, explaining about her latest fan fiction and asking Coco to convince Hayes to read it. And she couldn't keep quiet any longer. She'd seen the two together. Their chemistry was undeniable. They belonged together.

Hayes had to read the story, to hear Violet's apology, and to understand her side.

"Hayes?"

"Yup?"

"Violet just—"

Abruptly, Hayes stood up, his chair tumbling back behind him. He pulled it up, fumbling a bit and turning red around the ears. "Don't say her name, Coco. I don't want to hear it."

"But she just posted another story. This one isn't really fiction. You need to read it."

Hayes sat back heavily. "Not interested," he said shortly. "This is my thank-you snack, right, Coco? And if you want me to hang around for it, we'd better change the subject. So," he said, taking a deep breath, "are you taking Barry to the premiere tonight?"

"I tried," Coco said an hour later, talking to Violet on the phone. "But he wouldn't listen at all."

Violet squeezed her eyes shut. She'd been pacing the bedroom, her cell phone held tightly in her hand, waiting to hear from Coco. And now, she wished Coco had never called.

"It's okay," she choked out, even though it wasn't—not by a long shot. "I know you did your best."

"It's a lot for him to take in. I think he just wants space now. Maybe that will change."

"Maybe," Violet echoed, thinking she stood a better chance of winning an Academy Award for a script she hadn't written. But why bring Coco down, too? She hung up, expecting the tears to flow more than ever. That had been her last chance. And it was a major fail. But she was all cried out. Her eyes were dry, and her heart was still broken.

Hours passed with Violet barely leaving her bedroom. The room had grown dark, but Violet hadn't bothered turning on the light. She was holding a book, pretending to read, when Mia came in. Mia flipped the light switch.

Violet blinked in the sudden brightness.

"Hey! I appreciate you embracing the casual Venice vibe, but you can't wear that to the premiere."

Violet gazed down at her outfit, an old pair of sweats with a soft stretched-out T-shirt—comfort clothes. "I wasn't planning to even wear this out of the house. I don't think I'm going. Hayes doesn't want to see me. He doesn't even want to hear my name! I don't want to upset him any more than I already have."

Mia sat down on the edge of the bed. "You really should

go, Violet. It's your movie, too. You put so much work into it this summer. You deserve to be there just as much as anyone else. I think if you missed it, you'd always regret it."

"What about Hayes?"

"These things are always jam-packed. And that mansion is huge. You can avoid him. It wouldn't be that hard."

Without waiting for a reply, Mia opened Violet's closet door and went through dresses. She pushed hanger after hanger along the rack, rejecting each one. "Too young. Too old. Too creased."

Abruptly, she stopped near the end. "Oh! Where'd you get this?"

Violet sat up. "Coco must have left it that time she came here with her team."

The dress was lovely, bright yellow and strapless, not quite long enough to be a gown, with a bubble hem gathered at the bottom, and much shorter in the front than the back. Eye-catching, yet not overly dramatic.

Violet thought about *The Midnight Hawk*, all the scenes, all the actors, all the work. She didn't want to wait and see the movie in any old theater. She wanted to see it with the cast and crew—right now.

"It was just amazing!" Violet stood next to Coco, gazing at the glittering crowd in the ballroom-like space, all chattering excitedly about the movie. "I swear, I knew what was going to happen, but I was still on the edge of my seat the whole time. You were awesome, Coco."

Coco grinned. "I'm so happy with the way it turned out. You know, I think TJ was crying at the end!"

"That final scene was heartbreaking." Violet had hated to think about going over those lines with Hayes, trying to help him and feeling so close. But she couldn't tear her eyes away from the screen. "The way you walked away, keeping your back straight while you were falling apart, was absolutely on-target."

Coco squeezed her hand. "I'm glad you came, Violet. And look around. It's wall-to-wall people here. You don't have to see anybody you don't want to see."

"Hi, Coco. Violet," Tez said, walking over. Violet sucked in her breath.

"Can I talk to you?" he asked Violet.

Before Violet could open her mouth, Coco spoke quickly. "Sure. I see Barry over there. Catch you later, Violet." Coco squeezed her hand one more time, then disappeared into the crowd.

"Well, you made it here," Tez told Violet. "I was afraid you wouldn't come."

"It was a hard decision," she acknowledged.

"It took courage. It's good you're here. You should be. You worked hard, and it's time to celebrate." He looked

Violet steadily in the eye. "I'm glad I got to know you over the summer. I don't think you ever intended to hurt Hayes."

Violet breathed a sigh of relief.

"You were good for him, Violet. He never would have nailed that emotional ending if you weren't helping him."

"Thanks, Tez. I hope things work out with Mia." Ever since Hayes had frozen her out, Mia hadn't mentioned Tez at all. But Violet knew the two had been seeing each other. She gave Tez a hug. "Take care."

"You, too, V."

Violet smiled, glad that some peace had been made.

When Tez left, Violet stood alone, feeling awkward. She didn't see anyone she knew. But she remembered Mia's parting words: "When you don't know what to do, head for the food." The table was along the wall, not too far away. Violet took her time walking over.

She hadn't gotten far when a hand reached out to stop her.

"Well, as I live and breathe, it's Violet Reeves."

"Lydia Jacobs."

Violet had avoided Lydia's calls and texts. She hadn't known what to say, or how she felt, or what should be done.

"You haven't been in touch." Lydia's tone softened. "I don't blame you. I'm sorry I told TJ you were the mystery writer. But he wanted to do a project based on the stories.

And if I hadn't told him, he would have moved on to something else."

"But—"

Lydia held up her hand. "I know what you're going to say. TJ is hard to work with. He's difficult. All that is true. Yet he's also the best young director in Hollywood. I didn't want you to miss out on the opportunity to work with him at a higher level."

"That's not what I was going to say," Violet interrupted. "I know TJ, his good points and bad. I understand your reasons, and at first I gave you a pass. But I wanted you to keep it quiet so I'd have time to talk to Hayes. You didn't, and I hurt someone I care about. I wouldn't have done any of this on purpose—knowingly cause someone pain just to get ahead. But I think you would."

She looked Lydia square in the eye. "I don't want to work with you. Our deal is over."

Lydia's mouth dropped open; the great and powerful Lydia Jacobs had just been fired.

Violet nodded once, then continued on to the food table. She felt strong; she felt good. She'd probably burned a major bridge; she couldn't disregard the fact that Lydia was, in fact, a big Hollywood player. And now she'd surely refuse to work with Violet again. She could spread the word around town: Stay away from Violet Reeves. She's bad news.

No matter what, though, it was the right thing to do.

Violet took a plate and looked over the table, trying to decide between the dishes, when a roar erupted in the room. She stood on her tiptoes, peering over heads. Then she gasped. Hayes had just stepped onto the stage. He adjusted the mic.

People clapped and cheered and whistled. Slowly, Violet turned away from the food, her stomach in knots. She'd lost her appetite, but she still gripped the plate tightly, glad to have something solid to hold.

Hayes looked so adorable, wearing that very same outfit they'd chosen together, this time with a classic fedora on his head and dark green sneakers. She hadn't seen him in weeks. Somehow she expected him to look different. Older, maybe, or hardened. But he looked exactly the same: smiling, sweet, and cute.

"Settle down, everyone!" Hayes called out good-naturedly. Immediately, the crowd quieted. "I'd just like to say a few words, if you don't mind."

"We don't mind!" a young production assistant called out, and a wave of laughter swept the room.

"Good," Hayes continued. "So first I want to thank—"

"The Academy," the same production assistant shouted. "For this very special award, my very first Oscar. You deserve it for this role, Hayes!"

Everyone murmured in agreement.

"Cut it out, Simon!" Hayes grinned. "I want to thank

everyone involved in *The Midnight Hawk*." He paused. "Even you, Simon!"

People hooted.

"Seriously, all the PAs, Jon the gaffer, the craft service people, with a special shout-out to Simone, who made sure we always had a supply of cupcakes."

"Hear, hear," someone shouted.

Violet had pressed closer to the stage for a better look. At the word *cupcakes*, though, she froze, a picture flashing in her mind of the two of them, laughing as they made cupcake sandwiches.

Hayes went on, thanking just about everyone in the cast and crew. *How did he do it?* Violet wondered. He remembered each and every person's name. She held her breath each time he said a name, thinking now . . . now he'd mention her. He never did.

Hayes ended with TJ, saying, "And last, but certainly not least, a great big thank-you to our fearless director. Long may he reign! You all made my first movie the best it can be, and I couldn't possibly be more appreciative."

Another round of applause interrupted the speech. Hayes waited a moment.

"I'm going on tour tomorrow, and our work is done. But I'll never forget a single moment of filming. I'll always treasure the experience."

People raised their arms over their heads to clap even louder.

Violet turned away, certain the speech was over. That was it. The last she'd see of Hayes Grier.

"But before I go," Hayes added, his voice rising over the noise, "there's something I have to straighten out." He held a hand over his eyes to look out over the room. "Violet Reeves, can you join me onstage?"

PART FOUR

Girl Gets Boy?

CHAPTER TWENTY-ONE

WHAT? HAYES WANTED HER to join him onstage? Shocked beyond belief, Violet dropped her plate. It bounced on the carpet, and a waiter quickly scooped it up.

"Violet?" Hayes called again.

"She's right over there!" Simon shouted, pointing.

Heads turned, and everyone stared at Violet, standing awkwardly, not even a plate to hold on to for security. The sea of people parted, and Violet had no choice but to walk unsteadily to the stage. Helping hands boosted her up. She stood next to Hayes, her heart beating wildly.

What would Hayes say next? That she was a traitor, a

rat, the worst sort of hanger-on, out only for herself? She trembled and waited, steeling herself to hear the worst.

"As I said," Hayes said, not looking at her but at the audience. "I know our work is done. But I couldn't walk away without saying something about this girl right here."

Violet swayed a bit, then steadied herself.

"She was the one who helped me run lines all during the shoot. And I need her help one last time."

What was Hayes talking about? For the first time, Violet noticed he held two scripts. He handed one to her.

It was titled, *Shooting Stars at Midnight*, written by Hayes Grier.

Finally, Hayes looked at her, and he smiled. Violet's heart melted. She flipped to the next page and scanned it quickly. The screenplay told their story, the story of Violet and Hayes.

It began with Hayes joking around with his buddies in the trailer, and Violet accidentally saying, "I love you."

Now she had to say it again, as one of her lines. She managed but just barely, and the crowd cracked up.

The next scene was at the cupcake shop. Hayes had a few lines listing Violet's favorite—and weird—cupcakes, which got increasingly stranger. The last one he said was mint-onion dip, mixed with pepper, topped with a dollop of wasabi sauce. "That was one hot cupcake," he added.

The crowd groaned, and Violet tried to control her giggles.

They turned another page and reached the part where Hayes found out Violet had written the fan fiction: He hadn't wanted to talk to her and didn't answer her texts when she tried to apologize.

"Yeah," Violet said, reading her line. "That was pretty rude."

They looked at each other and laughed.

Hayes recited, "But I had to forgive you. Because ever since we shared those cupcakes, I knew you were the one."

"You did?" Violet squeaked, going off-script. She lifted her eyes to meet his, her heart fluttering, and her knees weak.

Hayes motioned to her to keep reading. Violet turned the page. "To be continued . . ." she said out loud, "by Hayes Grier and Violet Reeves."

Wait. What?

The crowd fell silent, looking up at the stage.

Violet leaned in to whisper in Hayes's ear. "What happens next?"

Hayes shrugged in his usual cool-guy way, and Violet's heart leaped. "We haven't finished our story yet. You're the writer, V. Can you help me with the ending?"

"So it's okay? We're okay?"

Hayes pulled her close. "What do you think?"

She smiled at him, a smile so full of love, she thought the people in the very back of the room could feel it, too. Sometimes life really could be like a boy-meets-girl movie, complete with happy ending.

Hayes smiled back. And then Violet didn't notice anything else . . . not the cheers . . . not the people . . . only Hayes . . . Hayes, Hayes, Hayes . . . as they kissed.

TURN THE PAGE *for*
A BONUS Q&A
and MORE!

EXCLUSIVE FAN Q&A WITH HAYES

If you could be a cartoon character for a week, who would you be? —Jaden
No doubt, Superman. I'd love to fly.

Where do you see yourself in ten years? —Persja
Being in more films, producing series and films, being a part owner of an NFL team, and having my own clothing line.

What is the scariest thing you've ever done? —Sofia
Lean out of a helicopter that was 200 feet off the ground. It was thrilling!

If you could save one thing in a fire, what would it be? —Mia
Zan. My dog is my son.

Where is your favorite place to travel? —Kayla
Hawaii.

What's your favorite gas station snack? —Madeleine
Boiled peanuts.

If you could give yourself some advice when you started all this, what would it be? —Shahirah
Be humble, work hard.

What is one thing that always reminds you of home? —Izabelle
When I go for a hike with Zan in the woods, it feels a bit like Carolina.

What are the three things you're most thankful for in life? —Mirta
My family, Zan, and my amazing fans.

What's your favorite thing about meeting fans and traveling around the world? —Jessica
Feeling the love from my fans and exploring places neither I nor my family ever thought we would see.

HAYES'S PERFECT DAY

My book takes place over twelve days and twelve nights. But what would I do if I could have one perfect day? Here's my ideal day, from morning to night.

9 AM: I wake up and immediately down a fresh glass of OJ. There's nothing like a good, strong dose of vitamin C to get you going in the morning. OJ gives me the energy I need to start my day.

11 AM: I take my dog Zan on a walk on the beach, where we play fetch. I love living in LA because the beach is only a short drive away. I adopted Zan from a shelter in 2015, and he's my best friend. It's a blast watching him grow up and learn new things. Zan even has his own Instagram account, @ZanthePup. I help him run the account.

1 PM: I meet my friend Tez Mengestu at Chipotle for a quick bite to eat. Tez and I have been friends for a while, and it's nice to catch up and see what he's up to. Tez is from North

Carolina, like me, and it's nice to have someone to talk to about home and what it's like living in LA.

3 PM: Tez and I meet our crew for hoops at a local park. Even after eating a huge burrito, I school all of them. No one can keep up with me on the court, but it's fun to watch them try. And fail.

5 PM: I play with Zan in my backyard. Zan loves to play fetch. He's still a puppy, so he has a ton of energy. After our basketball game, I get tired out before he does!

7 PM: I get dinner at Buffalo Wild Wings. I never get sick of wings, and Buffalo Wild Wings has more than twenty flavors, so it's the perfect spot for me to get food at the end of an active day. I don't like to cook, so LA is perfect for me. There's so much good food, and everyone loves to eat out.

11 PM: After a busy day, I crash at home. I might watch a movie or binge-watch one of my favorite television shows. Tomorrow, I get to do this all again. I'm living my dream.

FAMILY ALBUM

This is our Hallmark shot! Me, Nash, and Will — three country boys on the train tracks.

Me with my brothers, Nash and Will, on our dirt bikes. I still love dirt biking.

Me and my brother Nash at the skate park. We loved to skate pools!

My stepdad, Johnny, made me this homemade surfboard.

Game break! Nash and I are discussing a scoring drive.

Me and my little sister, Skylynn, at a parade.

Fishing with Johnny!

Skiing in North Carolina. I love being outdoors.

Me and Mom on the lake. My mom is still my biggest fan.